Rockett's World

WHO'S RUNNING THIS SHOW?

Read more about

Rockett's World
in:

#1 WHO CAN YOU
TRUST?
#2 WHAT KIND OF
FRIEND ARE YOU?
#3 ARE WE THERE
YET?
#4 CAN YOU KEEP A
SECRET?
#5 WHERE DO YOU
BELONG?
#6 WHO'S
RUNNING THIS
SHOW?

Purple Moon

Rockett's World

WHO'S RUNNING
THIS SHOW?

Lauren Day

SCHOLASTIC INC.

New York Toronto London Auckland Sydney
Mexico City New Delhi Hong Kong

ISBN 0-439-08695-7

12 11 10 9 8 7 6 5 4 3 2 1   0 1 2 3 4 5/0

Printed in the U.S.A.   40
First Scholastic printing, May 2000

Rockett Movado sat in the school cafeteria, her chin propped in one hand while the other hand pushed a forkful of wilted lettuce around her plate.

Across the table, her freckle-faced friend Jessie was crunching through salad like a power mower. "I was thinking maybe I'd play my flute. If I can get up the nerve to audition," Jessie said, spearing a tomato wedge. "Do you think that would be too boring?"

Before Rockett could say go for it, Jessie called out to Ruben Rosales, "So are Rebel Angels gonna rock the talent show?"

Rebel Angels was Ruben's band. And Ruben, all cute and casual, with thick, dark hair and mischievous black eyes, was the homeroom hottie Rockett was kinda crushed on.

"*Hola, chicas*," he greeted them. "I'm going solo this year. I'm working on this monster guitar riff that'll end the show in a blaze of blown minds and burned-out amps."

"That sounds fun," Jessie said. "Doesn't it, Rockett?"

"Fully," Rockett agreed, happy for Ruben — and for Jessie — but feeling way weirdly gloomy-girl herself.

All week long, the buzz at Whistling Pines Junior High had been about the upcoming eighth-grade talent show. Kids were radically psyched, rehashing last year's most memorable moments and making plans for what they'd do this time.

Now the entire eighth grade was scheduled to meet in the auditorium after lunch to hear Ms. Tinydahl, the show's adviser, and Mr. Baldus, its emcee-to-be, talk about putting it together. Everywhere you went, from homeroom to lunchroom, everyone was pumped.

Except me, Rockett thought. *I have lots of talent, but no idea what to do for the show.*

If only I were musical like Jessie and Ruben. Or good at drama. Or dancing. Or gymnastics. I don't even own a singing dog!

I'm good at drawing but this time all I'm drawing is a blank.

"Hey, my man Rosales! What cooks?" Wolf DuBois, one of Ruben's pals, high-fived him.

Glinting against Wolf's black T-shirt, Rockett could see the Arctic wolf's tooth his Native American grandfather had given him. Wolf wore it on a leather cord around his neck. "The closest I ever got to performing was dancing and drum beating at a Pawnee powwow my dad took me to."

"That would be choice," Rockett said, "to do a Native American thing for the talent show."

Wolf shrugged. "I guess," he said unenthusiastically.

Whoops, Rockett thought. *That's how much I know about talent shows.*

"What are you guys going to do?" he asked, swiftly shifting attention away from himself.

"I might play the flute," Jessie answered.

Rockett just shrugged.

"Cool," Ruben noted. Then he and Wolf moved on.

"Cool?" Rockett murmured when they were out of earshot. "What's so cool about I don't know what to do?"

"Hey, Jessie. Hi, Rockett." Arrow Mayfield nodded at them, setting her single long feather earring fluttering. Friendly and confident, Arrow was flanked by the members of her all-girl band, Viva Cortez and Ginger Baskin.

"So are you guys auditioning for the show?" Jessie asked them.

"Together? No." Ginger shook her head. "Ruben's got the lock on rock this year."

"So we're just gonna do our own things," Arrow said. "Separately. Like Ginger's uncle sent her this excellent bagpipe from Scotland —"

"My uncle Frankie," Ginger explained. "He's the one who nicknamed me Ginger because of my red hair. He taught me to play a couple of songs on it."

"I'm going to dance," Viva announced, drumming a flourish with her fingertips on the molded plastic tabletop.

"You play drums *and* you dance?" Rockett was impressed.

"She also plays the xylophone, cymbals, maracas, and castanets. Viva's loaded with talent," Arrow said.

"What about you?" Ginger teased and turned to face Rockett. "Arrow plays the drums, too, our gifted Cherokee leader —"

"Part Cherokee," Arrow corrected her. "I'm also German and Welsh."

"Arrow's a drum-banging, in-line-skating, guitar-strumming, songwriting, keyboard-slammin', soul-singing, volleyball-playing archery buff," Viva declared, spinning so her Indian print skirt flared freely. The slim, dark-haired girl was always in motion, moving to some rockin' inner beat.

"Whew," said Jessie, "so are you gonna sing, play, or skate at the tryouts?"

"Actually, I'm thinking of doing an archery demonstration," Arrow confided. "See you guys in the auditorium after lunch."

"Archery. Dance. Bagpipe." Rockett's head was reeling as the trio took off. "Wow, that crew's really got it going on in the talent department. No wonder there's none left over for me."

Jessie wasn't buying it. "Rockett, that is so not true," she gently scolded. "You're one of the most talented people I know. I mean, you're great at art. You're a wonderful photographer. You take amazing pictures."

"Oh, right. I can't wait to audition. You think I should use my flash or just take regular snaps? Or maybe," Rock-

4

ett said, trying to make a joke of it, "I could go Polaroid and really amaze everyone."

Jessie's giggle was practically drowned out by a burst of sarcastic laughter. "Rockett Movado, camera girl. Oh, that would totally wow the crowd."

Nicole Whittaker was the head of The Ones, Whistling Pines's most popular crew. She and her best buds, Stephanie and Whitney, were cruising by the table, holding lunch trays.

"You're going to take pictures for the talent show?" Whitney asked, braces glinting against her white teeth.

"I was kidding," Rockett said. "I don't know what I'm going to do yet."

"Well, you can try out whatever lame act you want," Nicole informed her. "It won't make any difference, 'cause The Ones have got the totally dopest act."

"We do?" Whitney asked.

"Definitely," Nicole confirmed. "I'm working out this stellar cheerleading routine for you, me, and Steph."

"I don't think so," Stephanie said, sounding nearly as glum as Rockett felt. "I've so got nothing to cheer about."

"Don't worry, Stephanie." Shifting her tray to one hand, Whitney patted her dejected pal's shoulder. "Panama will be all right."

"Panama?" Jessie asked.

"Get over it, Stephanie," Nicole ordered. "He's just a bird."

"A bird?" Jessie said.

"A parrot," Nicole snapped at Jessie, "like some people I could mention!"

"He's not *just a bird*," Stephanie objected as Jessie blushed. "He's my pet, and there's something wrong with him. I'm sorry, Nic. I'm way too bummed to care about a dumb class talent show."

"Dumb?" Nicole snarled. "You can't mean the very same talent show for which I furiously sacrificed my precious time and energy last year, the very show that would have failed had I not given so generously of myself —"

"The only thing she gave generously of was her *mouth*," Dana St. Clair cracked. "If it wasn't issuing orders, then it was dissing everyone in sight." The peppery redhead was walking by the table with her bests, Miko Kajiyama and Nakili Abuto. The trio made up the CSGs, or Cool Sagittarius Girls.

"Excuse me?" Nicole glared at Dana.

"Well, it's true." Nakili stood by her pal. "You were totally bossy."

"Tyrannical rex," Miko quipped, signaling her buds to move on.

"Whatever," Nicole dismissed them. "My point is, would a sulky parrot have stopped me from whipping a bunch of kids into a disciplined cast? Or from joining my loyal friends in a showstopping number? Not even!" Handing Whitney her tray, she took Stephanie's arm and led her friends away.

"Nicole was the stage manager for last year's talent

6

show. It's really like being Ms. Tinydahl's student assistant, but they call it stage manager," Jessie filled Rockett in. "She was supposed to help. You know, like make sure everyone who wanted to be in the show got to audition and that the acts didn't run too long and that kids had stuff they needed. But Nakili was right. Nic was totally bossy. And she'd embarrass kids, cut down their acts in front of everyone else. It was a disaster."

"Forsooth and forsythia, shall I guess of whom thou speakest?" His Geekness Arnold Zeitbaum flung his skinny self into the chair next to Rockett's. "Couldst it be Nicole the knuckleheaded, yon damsel of destruction, the girl who dished out more shame-and-blame last year than Marty's Beef sold burgers?"

Jessie laughed. "Hey, Arnold," she said.

"Are you trying out for the show this year?" Rockett asked him.

"Ah, fair maidens, how auspicious is thy question," he said. "I'm polishing up a stratospherically superb magic act, mind-boggling feats of prestidigitation, complete with disappearing doves and silk scarves streaming from unsuspecting ears. Yet 'twill be for naught if I don't find the magician's assistant of my dreams."

"What kind of assistant are you looking for?" Jessie asked.

"My needs are meager — I'm looking for a delectable damsel babe — one such as yourselves, who might do justice to the spangly golden costume that I have in mind."

"Yeech!" The interruption came from Mavis Wartella-

Depew. "I can't believe even my own two good ears that you're going to try once more, Zit-wit, to trot out that ripe Houdini act again after your match trick fizzled so grievously last year."

Although he was sitting and Mavis was standing with her arms crossed, Arnold made it seem as if he were looking down his nose at her. "Be gone, wretch," he ordered.

"Be gone yourself, toadhead," Mavis shot back. "I was considering, just for one teeny fragment of a laughable lost second, telling you that I happen to know where such a flashy costume might be found. But now, mangled mind-clot, you're all alone on your own."

"Mavis," Rockett asked, trying to distract the irritated girl, "what are you going to do in the show?"

"She'll probably try some pathetically played-out mind-reading act," Arnold claimed. "Madame Wartella-Depew-trid is a master at telling the future — *after* it happens."

Ignoring Arnold, Mavis drew herself up indignantly. "Gifted though I am in sensitivity and foresight, I don't do cheap tricks with my exceptional intuitive talents," she declared.

"So you're saying you're not going to participate?" Rockett asked.

"Not unless I find a task worthy of my gifts," Mavis answered.

Oh, great. That'll make two of us. Just me and Mavis sitting on the sidelines, watching all the fun.

"What about you, Rockett?" the mystic demanded. "What special talents are you going to showcase?"

Rockett sighed. "None, I guess. I mean, I don't have any."

"Don't listen to her," Jessie insisted. "She can do lots of things."

"Rockett's gifts are un-doubtless," Mavis agreed. "And probably far better than some of the pitiable pod people among us who only *wish* they were as talented as they think they are. Well, see you in the auditorium." With a wave, she left them.

"Hey, Your Exalted Mumbo-jumbo-ness," Arnold called, hurrying after her. "Wait, hold up, hang on. You don't really know where to snag a sequined bodysuit, do you?"

"It's true, Rockett," Jessie said as soon as they were alone. "You really are gifted. And there's lots you could do. Like you could use your art and photo talents to design posters promoting the event. You're, like, the best artist. And advertising is way important to the talent show's success."

Sure, I could do that. I could even take pictures of the performers for the school paper. But it's so not what I had in mind. I mean, it wouldn't exactly get me a lot of applause.

Jessie's right that it's something I'm good at. And it's definitely something the show needs.

But I'd rather do something onstage, just like everybody else.

9

Confession Session

It's weird how sometimes you can know a person better than she knows herself. Rockett's a natural to head up the publicity committee. I can't believe she's not jumping at the chance. She's smart, cool, creative, helpful, fun, and an excellent artist. But it's like she doesn't even realize what she has to offer.

CHAPTER TWO

The auditorium was jammed with kids jogging back and forth across the aisle or turned around in their seats, teasing one another about who was going to have the wickedest act in the show.

Ms. Tinydahl, in a ruffly blouse and flowing floral skirt, was on the stage with Mr. Baldus, who was wearing his ancient flared-bottom jeans and a weird yellow shirt with billowing sleeves. They were studying a clipboard and seemed oblivious to the chaos raging around them.

Up onstage with them Rockett saw Darnetta James. Darnetta was Jessie's friend but she clammed up and acted all moody whenever Rockett was around. About all they had in common was that they both liked Jessie — they didn't click with each other.

Rockett wondered what Darnetta would do for the show. She didn't even know what Darnetta's talents were.

She and Jessie made their way down the crowded aisle, looking for seats. Rockett suddenly thought of something. "You see how the auditorium is right now — all hyper and full of color and noise like a giant circus? Wouldn't that be a cool way to do the posters? Circus style. Or like an ad for some monster rock event. Maybe I should do publicity after all."

"You're amazing." Jessie beamed at her. "You see things I'd never notice. I know you're the right person. You could do the best job ever."

Just then, Darnetta hurried down the steps of the stage. "Jessie, guess what?" she called. "I just spoke to Ms. Tinydahl about heading up the poster effort!"

"What's that mean . . . um, exactly?" Rockett asked with a sinking feeling.

"Oh, hi," Darnetta said coolly. "It means I'm in charge of promoting this year's show. I'm head of the committee that'll design ads and posters and announcements and invitations." She turned to Jessie again, adding, with a lot more excitement in her voice, "And I'm going to be the official photographer, too."

"Gee, 'Netta," Jessie said, glancing anxiously at Rockett.

Oh, no, Rockett thought. *It's bad enough that Darnetta moved in on the one job I'm qualified for, but I hate it when Jessie gets all nervous about me.*

I hope she doesn't try to make everyone feel better now. I can just imagine her going, "Isn't that great, Rockett? You can be on Darnetta's committee."

No way. Never. I mean, Darnetta's a decent artist and everything. But she's also got a neat voice and knows a lot about music. So why isn't she singing? Why did she have to go after the one job I could do?

"Whew, Darnetta," Rockett said quickly. "You jumped right in there, didn't you?"

"Thanks," Darnetta said. Then she hugged Jessie, who finally grinned and said, "Excellent, 'Netta. I'm so happy for you."

As Darnetta hurried up the aisle (to assemble a team, she told them), Rockett and Jessie finally found some seats near the front.

"Are you okay?" Jessie asked.

"Fine," Rockett said, slumping down in her seat.

"You're not," Jessie protested. "I can tell. I'm sorry —"

"What are you sorry about? It was a good idea. I was starting to get psyched for it. But it's just bad luck."

"You could still work with 'Netta," Jessie ventured, but one look at Rockett's expression changed her mind. "Or not. Anyway, it could be good luck. I mean, maybe you wouldn't have enjoyed it that much. Or maybe something better will come up."

Jessie's optimism, which Rockett usually admired, was really annoying right now. "Like what?" she couldn't help grumbling. "Heading up the cleanup crew? Sweeping the stage between performances? What else am I so perfectly cut out for?"

"All right now, *silencio*, troubadors and thesbians," Ms. Tinydahl trilled from the stage. "Quiet, please."

"Settle down, all you swingin' chicks and crazy cats, so we can get this happening happenin'," Mr. Baldus boomed, grinning.

"Chicks and cats?" Jessie giggled. "You saw a circus, but Mr. Baldus sees a farm."

"Swingin' chicks? Gag me," Nicole crabbed as she and her posse parked themselves behind Rockett and Jessie. "Where does he come up with this stuff?"

"Welcome. Welcome, everyone. We only have a few minutes and a lot to accomplish. Auditions will begin tomorrow," Ms. Tinydahl reminded them. "Today, we've got important positions to fill. Darnetta James has graciously volunteered to handle our advertising and promotion this year. Let's thank her, please."

There was a round of applause as Darnetta smiled shyly and waved from her seat.

"Anyone interested in working on that committee, please talk to her after homeroom. We also need a stage manager." Ms. Tinydahl paused for a second. "Does everyone know what a stage manager does?"

"Nag and insult people like Nicole did last year?" Dana called out.

"Tell everyone how badly their acts bite," Sharla Norvell sneered.

"Play favorites," someone else yelled.

"Be so bossy it makes you want to spew," Nakili offered.

"If only it were that easy!" Nicole called out. "Though it's by far the most important student position in the entire show, the stage manager has the thankless task of organizing everything. She makes sure people audition in an orderly way —"

"Yeah, right. Friends first, is that what you mean?" Ginger chuckled.

"And that everyone who wants to be in the show gets a chance to try out," Nicole continued, ignoring the interruption. "And that their acts aren't too long and that they have what they need to do their very best."

"I think Nicole did a brilliant job last year," Stephanie affirmed, snapping out of her bird funk to support her bud.

Whitney stood suddenly. "I nominate Nicole Anne Whittaker as stage manager *again* this year," she declared.

Suddenly, the room was filled with boos, catcalls, and snickers. Kids were yelling, "No way." "Forget it." "I am so outta here!"

"Excuse me," Nicole shouted. "Hello? Did I say I wanted to do it again?"

Rockett thought she'd seen Nicole wince at the back-biting blitz but the leader of The Ones quickly moved on.

"Being your stage manager was a tremendous challenge — which I more than met!" the audacious girl continued. "But, while I wish to thank *all* my loyal supporters for their kudos and confidence, I must decline your kind offer."

"There you go," Jessie whispered to Rockett, "there's a job you could totally ace. You're a really good organizer. Plus you're friends with lots of different kids so you wouldn't play favorites. And you'd never be as mean or bossy as Nicole was. Honestly, Rockett, you ought to volunteer for stage manager. Nicole's right about one thing. It's about the most important job there is."

"Now the torch must be passed to a new generation," Nicole continued.

"I'll do it," Arnold said.

Nobody paid any attention.

"The time has come to find a new person," Nicole went on, scanning the auditorium, "to take my place. As if anyone could."

As her eyes fell on various kids, they cringed and slid lower in their seats.

"A *student* . . . willing to try — to meet the high standard I set."

"She is so looking for someone to fail," Dana said.

"Did you just volunteer?" Nicole nailed her.

"Not even!" Dana declared.

Suddenly, Nicole eyed Rockett. "Hmmm," she murmured thoughtfully. "Speaking of new. How about you, Movado?"

"Nic, don't," Whitney whispered.

"Why not? I nominate Rockett Movado as this year's stage manager."

"Yessss!" Jessie shouted, thrusting her fist in the air.

"Excellent," Miko agreed. "Rockett would make a choice stage manager."

"She might even be fair," Dana grudgingly admitted.

"Rockett for stage manager," Nakili joined in.

Arrow, Ginger, and Viva started chanting, "Rockett,

Rockett, Rockett," as Viva slapped the rhythm on the seatback in front of her.

"She'd be cool," Ruben agreed. When she glanced at him, he winked at her. "You can do it, *chica*."

Rockett could feel herself redden. "Me?" she whispered to Jessie.

"Well, they don't mean your sister, Juno," Jessie teased.

Juno? The mention of her older sib stopped Rockett cold. Juno was perfect. If you wanted to feel small or inadequate, all you had to do was hang with her. But, being flawless, Juno wouldn't let that happen. She'd pump you up with pep talk till your bruised ego was fully bloated again.

Rockett loved the girl, but hated being compared to her.

"Now *she* would be the perfect stage manager," Rockett responded, only half-joking.

"Maybe, but you're the one we want," her loyal pal insisted. "Come on, girlfriend. Go for it."

Oh, wow. Stage manager. Jessie says it's a really big deal. Ruben's in my corner. And I'm blown away that so many kids think I'd be good at it.

But I'm not sure what I'd have to do.

And if Nicole did such a whack job last year, can I seriously do it better?

Plus, didn't Dana say Nicole's only looking for someone to fail?

"Well, what do you say, Rockett?" Mrs. Tinydahl was smiling expectantly.

"We don't 'draft' people into this army. We only accept volunteers," Mr. Baldus teased.

"Gee, I'd like to —" Rockett started to say.

Nicole interrupted, calling to the teachers, "I'd be happy to school her. You know, share my experiences and triumphs."

"That's very generous, Nicole," Ms. Tinydahl said. "Why don't the two of you take a moment to discuss the job at the back of the auditorium, while we move forward with other business?"

"Let's go," Nicole ordered with a jerk of her head. "Believe me, it's way simple — or I'd never have nominated you."

As Rockett made her way to the aisle, Jessie gave her a thumbs-up. "You'll be great," she promised. "You'll be the best stage manager ever."

"Okay, it's really no big deal," Nicole began when they reached the back of the room. "First and foremost, you're this junior assistant to Tinydahl and Baldus. You do their bidding. Their wish is your command. Of course, you also have a few chores of your own, like setting up the audition schedule so every wanna-be gets a chance to try out.

"Um, okay. I'm with you so far," said Rockett.

"You also time the tryouts. Let kids know when their acts are too long or short. You don't vote on who's in and who's out of the show but you do have influence. That's the best part: You can wheedle and whine at Ms. Tinydahl and Mr. Baldus until they see your point of view. I did. And very effectively, I think."

"Oh, I'm sure you were —" Rockett began reassuringly.

"So, after the powers-that-be make their selections," Nicole cut her off sharply, "you give the losers all these whack behind-the-scenes jobs like lighting, scenery, ushering, props. Tinydahl's got this tiny budget for costumes. Anyway, you're supposed to encourage volunteers for this stuff, but if nobody does, you just assign them. Baldus is very big on *everyone* participating. It's your responsibility to make sure every kid has something to do."

"Gee, that doesn't sound too hard," Rockett decided.

Nicole gave a bitter bark of a laugh. "You think it's easy telling kids that their acts are totally the same as the boring ones five other kids are planning? Or that their precious performances are running way overtime and they've got to kill the lame song or tired rap they wrote especially for the show?"

"Well, no, I didn't mean —"

"It's way harder than that. You've gotta be excellent at problem-solving. You've gotta practically be a genius to set up a decent audition schedule; and just when you think you've nailed it, Ruben's got band rehearsal or Ginger's got soccer practice the exact time they're slated to try out."

"That does sound complicated," Rockett said apologetically.

"To some people, I guess," Nicole replied. "It's no job for the weak and wussy. There's only one way to handle it. Get tough," she advised. "You've gotta show 'em who's boss right away."

"Well, I'm not sure I could —"

"Tough luck. That's how it is. It's either tough luck or tough love," Nicole insisted. "Oh, sure, you think they're your friends. They're all hot to cooperate. But tell them the truth — you know, like that the act they're all psyched about is terminally pathetic — and they'll turn on you. Try to be nice, honest, fair . . ." Nicole shook her head sadly. "They'll trash your show. Remember this, above all else, Rockett: It's lonely at the top."

"Um, well, okay. Thanks," she responded.

"No problem. Just take my advice and you'll do fine." Then Nicole sashayed back to her seat.

Rockett watched her go. *Whew. Is that really what it takes to do the job? If it is, I am so not going to volunteer. Yuck, I'd rather be weak and wussy than rude and bossy.*

I think Nicole's just bummed because nobody wants her in charge. It's probably because of all that "tough love" trash she was talking. Brrr. Could I even be that cold? No way. And what if I say yes and people don't like the way I do it? Then they won't like me, either.

Confession Session

I offered myself as stage manager and what did I get? Deaf ears and foul insults from the usual dolts. For none but fair Rockett would I step aside. Once she's in charge, she'll help me snag a righteous partner for my magic act. Like Whitney, for instance. In spangled costume and satin cape, that One would most excellently do.

I love Nicole to pieces, but she was way ripe as stage manager. I only nominated her again to squish her sulking. I hope she doesn't psych Rockett out. The new girl is so right for the job. Supportive yet undorky, not tied to any clique, she's an indie-girl who knows the value of teamwork. Yeeeuw! Why is Arnold Zitbomb staring at me?!

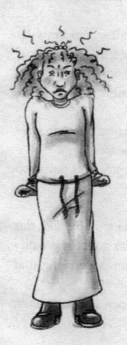

CHAPTER THREE

"I'm not sure Rockett-girl's got what it takes," Nicole was telling Whitney as Rockett returned to her seat.

"She'd never be as good as you," Whitney assured her bud.

The remark might have stung more if Whitney hadn't smiled at Rockett just then — and seemed genuinely friendly.

Rockett liked Whitney Weiss. She seemed more willing than the other Ones to break out once in a while and hang with kids who weren't walking designer labels. So it buoyed Rockett's spirit when Whitney added, "But she'd be okay."

As Rockett scooted into the row in front of them, she noticed Stephanie was slumped in her seat.

Jessie tugged at Rockett's sleeve. "So, are you going to do it?" she asked.

"The stage manager thing?"

Nicole thinks I'm not up to it. She made it sound like this dire chore. But if she went for it last year, it's gotta be a really choice thing to do; maybe even better than advertising and publicity.

It'd be cool to show Darnetta that I can do more than

make posters, too. And double cool to prove that Nicole's off base about me.

"It didn't sound all that hard," Rockett said. "And I wouldn't embarrass kids or do the kind of stuff Nicole did . . ."

"Never," Jessie agreed. "So does that mean yes?"

"I think so," Rockett decided.

Bo Pezanski, who was notorious for participating in as little as possible in school, including homework, leaned across Jessie unexpectedly. "Go for it, Red," he urged Rockett.

Onstage, Ms. Tinydahl was winding down her speech. "And this year, as usual, we're going to do what we've found works best. Mr. Baldus and I will choose the acts, based on variety. We don't want to have everyone doing the same things, so be creative with your talents — and, of course, time will be a factor, so try to keep your acts concise. Auditions begin on Thursday. And we'll have a Saturday session for those of you who have after-school activities during the week."

"Remember, not everyone will get to perform. This is Whistling Pines, not Woodstock," Mr. Baldus pointed out, his face crinkling. "But everyone gets to participate. And believe me, there'll be plenty to do — designing and making scenery, shopping for props . . ."

"Experience counts. I volunteer Nicole for shopping," Max Diamond teased.

Jessie giggled and Max grinned gratefully.

25

"I second that," Max's blond best, Cleve Goodstaff, Jr., added. "Nic's a monster shopaholic. She'd make a props prop girl."

"Vacuum-pack it, fools," Nicole snapped at her boy buds. "Shopping for talent show props is, like, grossly menial. And so secondhand. Finding thrift-shop hats and ratty old capes — it's simply heinous! I wouldn't do prop girl for a platinum credit card spree."

"Settle down, dudes and dudettes," Mr. Baldus urged. "You can sign up for dozens of noble activities as soon as we've got a stage manager. He or she will have the list of what we need."

"Go on," Jessie urged Rockett. "Volunteer."

Arrow, who was sitting in front of them, turned around. "Did you decide to do it?" she asked.

Rockett nodded yes. "I think so."

"Raise your hand," Jessie prompted her.

"Rockett's goin' for it!" Viva announced.

"Is that true?" Ms. Tinydahl asked.

"Um, well, yes," Rockett finally said.

"I totally had to talk her into it," Nicole claimed, but the remark was lost in a burst of cheers and congratulations for Rockett.

"Well, it's official." Ms. Tinydahl beamed from the stage. "We have our student assistant —"

"A.K.A. stage manager," Mr. Baldus added. "That's Also Known As —"

"A.K.A. Rockett Movado," Ruben hollered. "Nice going, *chica*! We gotta talk."

26

Darnetta called out, "I wanna sing this old blues number for the show but we've gotta find the sheet music first."

"Put me down for lighting chores," Chaz said. "I'd rather stay behind the scenes."

"Congrats, Rockett. As soon as you recruit a prop person, let me know," Ginger urged. "I'm going to do a Celtic bagpipe tune and I'm thinkin' I want, like, pots of shamrocks everywhere — you know, for atmosphere."

"You go, girl," Arrow hollered. "Can you find out if Mrs. Lutzi will lend me an archery target from PE? I mean, she'd say yes to the stage manager faster than she'd listen to me. It's no biggie. Just when you get a chance."

"I guess this lets you out as my magician's assistant," Arnold noted. "But I'm confident you'll help me win the perfect maiden for my act."

Rockett laughed. "Whoa," she said. "Hold on, you guys. Okay, so, Ginger, you want shamrocks. Ruben, give me a sec to get organized, okay! And Darnetta, can you write down the name of the song you need?"

Ms. Tinydahl cleared her throat. "All right, people. Let's contain our enthusiasm," she urged.

Mr. Baldus gave an earsplitting whistle. It cut through the rabble of demands, throwing the room into a momentary stunned silence. "Order in the auditorium!" he called.

"I'll have a chicken taco!" Ruben joked, making even Ms. Tinydahl smile.

"Whew, that was weird," Rockett confided to Jessie.

27

"They were just pumped, you know, happy that it's you, not Nicole," Jessie whispered. "Oooo, wait! Here comes Mr. Baldus. He's going to give you your clipboard."

Sure enough, Mr. Baldus was striding toward them, his ponytail bouncing, with a clipboard in his hand. "Rockett Movado, I now pronounce you stage manager," he teased.

Rockett glanced at some of the pages on the clipboard.

"That's the audition schedule right there on the top sheet." Mr. Baldus tapped the chart. "Just fill in the names next to the available times. We want everyone to have a chance to try out for the show."

"Definitely," Rockett agreed.

"And underneath the schedule," he said, flipping a page, "is a list of prime positions we'll want to fill. Darnetta will round up the ad and promo posse. The rest is up to you. But everyone's got to participate. If they're not performing, there are plenty other jobs to do."

Rockett nodded. She felt thirsty suddenly, but didn't want to interrupt Mr. Baldus.

Finally, he said, "Okey-dokey, Smokey. I think you're set for now. If you need anything else, come see me or Ms. Tinydahl. Any questions — catch us later. Congratulations again, Rockett." He grinned. "I know you'll be boffo!"

"Whew, I'm gonna get some water," Rockett told Jessie as Mr. Baldus raced back to the stage.

Clutching her clipboard, she hurried out of the auditorium and was on her way to the drinking fountain when she heard someone snuffling.

Stephanie was in the hall, leaning against her locker, looking way downhearted.

"Hi," Rockett said softly. "Um, anything I can do to help?" she asked, hugging the clipboard.

"Not unless you're a bird shrink," Stephanie answered glumly. "My parrot, Panama, is totally bummed and practically speechless. He's usually all talkative and full of life."

"That is so sad," Rockett agreed. "I wonder what happened?"

The clipboard felt a little like a shield, she noticed, protecting her but also allowing her to say things to Stephanie she wouldn't ordinarily have said. It was like their conversation was less personal, more . . . official. It was like: Stage Manager Rockett on the case.

Stephanie seemed to notice it, too. "Well, one thing," she answered thoughtfully. "My dad brought home this new kitten. Not to keep, just till it gets better."

Stephanie's father was a veterinarian, Rockett remembered.

"And I know it sounds mental," she continued, "but I think Panama got jealous. And that he's, like, sulking or something. He's very sensitive. And smart. But he wants to be in the spotlight all the time."

"The spotlight, huh?" Rockett mused. "Maybe he should be in the talent show."

She'd meant it as a joke, just to lighten things up with

Stephanie, but the melancholy girl blinked at her and, in a totally serious voice, said, "You really think so?"

All of a sudden, it didn't seem like such a bad idea.

"Well, you said he's smart and he can talk and everything."

"Well, I mean, he can say, 'Way,' 'Not even,' and 'I don't think so,'" Stephanie explained.

"And he loves to be in the spotlight. . . . I don't know," Rockett reasoned, "maybe you could do a bird act with him. Maybe it really would cheer him up to be the center of attention again."

"Omigosh, that is soooo brilliant!" Suddenly, Stephanie was hugging Rockett, crushing the clipboard against her ribs. "Thank you, thank you. I can't wait to tell Nicole and Whitney!" the grateful One gushed and rushed off.

Pleased with herself and basking in a do-good glow, Rockett headed for the water fountain. *Nicole was totally trying to scare me*, she decided. *Being a stage manager is a breeze, a no-brainer, the bomb. You're just the go-to girl in a jam. I can so do this!*

"So if anyone's interested in 'tech-ing' — which is what we call the technical and seriously important behind-the-scenes work," she heard Mr. Baldus announcing as she slipped back into the auditorium, "make sure you give your name to our capable new stage manager."

That's me, Rockett thought as she reached her row, *the answer girl!*

Nicole said a decent stage manager had to be excellent at

problem-solving. Well, I've already solved Stephanie's problem. And it's only Day One!

Of course, Nicole said I had to be tough, which I so don't believe. Courtesy and cooperation work a lot better than whipping kids into shape.

Okay, it was kind of scary when everyone was calling out their requests and demands. But it was exciting, too. Anyway, Ms. Tinydahl and Mr. Baldus got them to simmer down fast. So, no biggie. I can be helpful and supportive and leave the tough-love stuff to the teachers. They'll keep everyone in line.

All I have to do is stay cool, carry my clipboard, and keep coming up with choice solutions!

CHAPTER FOUR

"Are you all set now, dear?" Ms. Tinydahl called from the stage.

"I think so," Rockett answered, waving her clipboard.

"Okay, everyone. Ms. Tinydahl and I need to have a quick meeting before next period," Mr. Baldus announced. "So we'll be bookin', makin' tracks, cuttin' out. Give our new stage manager your full cooperation, please. You've got ten minutes before the end of the period. See Rockett to sign up for auditions. And good luck to all."

"Yeah, especially Movado," Rockett heard Nicole sneer. "Because she is so gonna need it."

Rockett glanced at Nicole and The Ones.

Stephanie's head was down. She wasn't looking all that psyched anymore.

Whitney's arms were folded sullenly across her chest.

Nicole was watching Rockett through narrowed eyes.

What's up with them? Rockett wondered. But there was no time to figure it out. The moment the teachers left, Rockett was swamped again.

Everyone in the entire auditorium seemed to be streaming into the aisles, funneling toward her. Kids were pushing, shoving, and shouting, "I want . . ." "I need . . ." "You gotta . . . "

Arnold was the first to reach her. "Here is the sublime costume my lucky assistant will require." He shoved a page torn from a magazine into her hand.

The outfit was dazzling, all spangly and sequined, and accessorized with glittery gold boots, a rhinestone headband, and a fun satin cape. "I'll take the first audition spot, plus I need a minute to talk with you now. *Privately*," he emphasized.

"Gee, Arnold" — Rockett motioned helplessly at the crowd of noisy kids surrounding them —"this isn't the best time."

"Oh, great! I thought we could work together —"

Rockett showed him the audition schedule. "See, I've got you down for first. And as soon as we have a prop person, I'll pass along your costume needs, okay?"

She was smiling as hard as she could, determined to be patient, polite, and encouraging.

"I thought you understood," he continued without glancing at the sheet, "that the only reason I withdrew as this year's stage manager was to support you so that you would support me. But I see your exalted position has already gone to your head."

"At least she's got a head for it to go to, Zit-wit." Mavis elbowed to the front of the mob. "Not like that numb knob on your neck."

"Honest, Arnold, I'll help you any way I can. But this

isn't exactly a private place," Rockett explained courteously.

With a sniff, the brainiac stalked away.

Rockett glanced at the schedule sheet on her clipboard. "Okay, Mavis, when do you want to audition?"

"Being too close to Zeit-clod must have messed with your mind, 'cause you are so in the vapor zone. I'm not interested in performing, Rockett. I thought I might sign up for something else."

"Oh, does it say, 'Nutcake needed' on that job sheet?" Dana cut in front of Mavis.

"Pathetic piglet," Mavis hissed, squinting wickedly at Dana. "Stinky soccer-ball breath."

"Ouch, that stings. Not." Dana rolled her eyes. "The CSGs want to audition last," she told Rockett. "We know we're gonna do something outstanding. We're just not sure what yet. So we need all the time we can get."

"Do something outstanding and disappear, Dana." It was Stephanie. "Rockett, as you know, I've *just* come up with an excellent idea for my act, so naturally I need time to develop it. Reserve a late slot for me, too."

"Um, okay, Stephanie, Dana. I'll pencil you guys in," Rockett said amiably. "And, Mavis, which job were you interested in?"

Mavis glanced around her. Dana and Stephanie were both regarding her with superior smirks. "I've changed my mind," she blurted. "I'm not wasting my gifts on pushy nincompoops or squandering my pearls on swine-

34

people." She wheeled away, almost bowling Ruben over as she crashed through the crowd.

"What's Mavis so hot about? Yo, and speakin' of hot, here's the thing, Rockett," he said. "I can't afford to destroy my amps. So I'm gonna need a new set. Well, a new *old* set. You know what I mean? Just some bad old amps I can explode at the end of my number."

Explode? Destroy? What is he talking about? And what are amps? Should I even ask or am I supposed to know?

Rockett could feel herself blushing. She'd ask Jessie later, she guessed. "Amps, sure. No prob, Ruben." Her smile was starting to feel a little frozen.

"Solid! I knew I could count on you."

"Music man." Ruben's pal Wolf slapped him five. "You are so going to blow everyone out of the water with that bad heavy-metal riff on your ax."

"Ax? Are you planning to chop up the . . ." Rockett checked her notes. "Um, the amps?"

Ruben and Wolf started laughing.

Arrow had overheard the exchange. "It's not that kind of ax," she explained.

"His ax means his instrument," Wolf clarified. "I was talking about Ruben's hot-wired bass."

Rockett looked helplessly at Arrow.

"Hot-wired bass equals electric guitar," Arrow said slowly. "Whew, I'm glad I'm not doing my music thing this year," she added as Wolf and Ruben took off together. "Ruben is way serious about his solo."

"And his *amps*," Rockett fished, hoping Arrow would tell her what they were.

Arrow didn't bite. "I guess," she said, shrugging. "Anyway, I don't care when you schedule my audition. I just hope you can talk Ms. Lutzi into lending me a target. Don't you think my idea of doing an archery exhibition is excellent? No one else is gonna go that route."

"Duh, of course not." Tugging Whitney along by the hand, Nicole had wormed her way to the front of the pack. "Because it's totally boring."

"It is not," Arrow snapped back. "It's cool, right, Rockett?"

"Well, it's . . . unique," Rockett hedged, determined to be supportive of Arrow, even though she sort of agreed with Nicole. An archery exhibition not only sounded like a snore, but kind of hazardous. Still, she was not going to trash Arrow's idea with everybody standing around listening. *That would be more Nicole's style than mine.*

"Speaking of cool, wait till you see my leotard." Viva was psyched. She and Jessie were wedged behind Whitney. "Well, it's a unitard, really. Long sleeves, full bodysuit. It's slinky black and moves so fine. It makes me look like panther girl, this total Catwoman. I'm going to dance in it to Darnetta's blues."

"And I might play the flute with them," Jessie confided.

"If we can find the song I want to do." Darnetta pushed past Nicole and thrust a scrap of paper into Rockett's hand. "It's called 'Delta Girl Blues' and it's on this, like, million-year-old record my mom has. But we need the sheet music. You gotta get it for us."

"Thanks for writing it down. But, well, Darnetta, I'm not sure where —" Rockett started to say.

"Hello. You *are* the stage manager," Nicole cut her off.

"And unless 'Netta gets the music, I've got nothing to dance to," Viva reminded her. "I mean, we could do a rough run-through without it, I guess —"

Who's responsible for getting the music? Rockett wondered. *And Ruben's amps? Is it the sound crew or the prop person?* "Okay, how about third slot tomorrow for the audition?" she asked.

"Cool. And then, if we're in, you'll find us the music," Darnetta said. "Thanks a bunch."

"See you later," Jessie called, and they were gone. Only Nicole, Whitney, and a dozen other frantic gimmes and I-needs remained.

"Delta Girl Blues," Rockett jotted the song title onto her notepad, then crumpled Darnetta's paper scrap. "Okay, you're up," she said, remembering to smile at Nicole and Whitney. "How can I help you guys?"

"She wants to know how she can help," Nicole repeated to Whitney. "Oh, let me see. How about talking our best friend into abandoning us? That would be helpful. You know, convince her, when she's desperate and weak with worry over her pitiful parrot, that what she ought to do is desert her posse and work up a duet with an emotionally disturbed bird."

"We'd like to audition tomorrow," Whitney said frostily, "like around three."

"No way!" Ginger hollered. "That's the only time I'm available."

"Excuse me, but three P.M. is mine. It's always mine," Sharla growled. "It was my audition slot last year, and I'm calling it again. No way am I hangin' around this joint a minute longer than I have to. And Saturday is so out."

"Who's doing the backdrops? Cleve and I are doing this stand-up routine, and I want a background that looks like a brick wall, you know, like all the comedy clubs have," Max informed her.

"Not even. It's gotta be black for my poetry reading," Sharla insisted. "A black curtain, you know, with, like, this one dramatic spotlight."

"Three tryouts at three o'clock. Black wall, bricks, got it." Rockett was scribbling as fast as she could, taking orders like a waitress.

I've got three people auditioning at the same time. Arrow's act, which I assured her was excellent, is either gonna put the audience to sleep or maim them. I just told Ruben I could score him a set of amps — forgetting to mention that I don't even know what they are. And where am I supposed to find a song sheet for Darnetta? At www.ijustdon'tknow.com?

Overwhelmed much?

Not even. I've just gotta figure out what to do first. What's most important?

That's easy. Not Darnetta! Except that if she doesn't get her music, Jessie and Viva are out of an act.

38

Get honest with Arrow and Ruben? And have them come down on me — like Nicole, Whitney, and Arnold already did? Not a priority.

Straighten out the audition schedule? There you go! That's what I'll do. Things'll be better once tryouts get going. . . .

CHAPTER FIVE

"Ruben Rosales, you're a total menace!" Nicole shrieked. "Do something, Rockett!"

Auditions were scheduled to begin in less than five minutes. The auditorium was rockin' with rowdy kids. Neither Mr. Baldus nor Ms. Tinydahl had shown up yet. And the paper airplane that Ruben had fired off to Cleve was sticking out of the salon-perfect 'do Nicole had gotten especially for her audition.

Whitney was trying to remove the missile without messing up her bud's hair. "This place is a zoo," she grumbled, while Nicole hopped around yelping, "Ow, ow, ouch!"

"Where are they?" Jessie whispered to Rockett.

"Baldus and Tinydahl? I don't know. I guess they're late."

"Brilliant, Movado!" Nicole remarked, batting away Whitney's hands. "You guess they're late. Duh. I can't believe I nominated you for stage manager."

"Rockett, check this out." It was Viva. The dancing drummer twirled to show off the black bodysuit she was wearing.

"Wow!" Rocket didn't know what she'd expected, but it wasn't head-to-toe spandex that fit like a second skin.

"It's amazing," she said. Viva looked fantastic, all long, muscular, and lean. "You really do look like Catwoman. That is truly slinky."

"It's fresh, right?" Viva said excitedly.

"Totally," Rockett agreed.

"No way is Ms. Prudey-doll gonna let you wear that sprayed-on suit," Dana declared.

"Put down that lame-o water gun, Max," Viva shouted suddenly. "You shoot one drop of slimy water onto my new costume, and I will so mess with you."

"Did you see that? He tried to hose her," Nicole reported to Arrow. "And what did Rockett do?"

"Rockett didn't do anything," Arrow replied calmly.

"Exactly!" Nicole took Rockett's arm and steered her toward the stage steps. "You get up there and make those jokers behave. Let them know who's in charge. It's your job."

Not!

"Please, Rockett," Viva implored, "I don't want Max trashing my unitard."

Or maybe it is . . .

Looking at the door, hoping to see Ms. Tinydahl or Mr. Baldus enter, Rockett reluctantly climbed onto the stage.

"Um, hello. Excuse me. Listen, everybody —"

A few kids in the front rows turned to listen to her. Sharla Rae Novell was one of them.

"Oh, no, here we go," Sharla griped. "It's Nicole the troll all over again."

"I am not!" Rockett insisted.

"That was cold," Whitney scolded her. "What's wrong with being Nicole?"

"Nothing," Rockett said weakly. "I meant about the troll part."

"Ignore her," Nicole ordered. "Max is still squirting people. Make him stop."

Rockett remembered to smile. "Um, okay, everyone. I mean, I just thought maybe we could go over the audition schedule . . . uh, you know . . . just till Ms. Tinydahl gets here."

"I'm up first!" Arnold called out.

"He is," Rockett said.

"As if!" Nicole barked. "Like Whitney and I are really going to follow you and your whack pigeons!"

"They're doves," Arnold asserted.

"Doves, shmoves, are they potty-trained? I think not. We go first."

"Sorry, Your Pushiness, but your reign of pain is over," Arnold insisted as a paper airplane sailed past him and looped upward, hitting Rockett's cheek.

Arnold snorted with laughter.

"It's not funny," Rockett grumbled.

"Oh, how awful." Nicole smirked. "Who threw that?"

"He did!" Cleve and Ruben shouted simultaneously, pointing at each other and cracking up.

"Cut it out, Ruben," Rockett said, stroking her cheek.

"Me? I didn't even throw it!" Ruben groused.

"It was Cleve," Max volunteered.

"I don't care who it was!" Rockett fumed. "You guys are acting really stupid. Throwing stuff and playing with water guns!"

"Ooooo, she's steamed." Dana giggled. "Watch out, people. Getting the stage manager all mad. She'll ax your acts."

A couple of kids laughed at that. Ruben didn't. He turned away from Rockett, shaking his head angrily.

"Sheesh, it's worse than having a teacher in the room," Max grumbled to Jessie.

How did I get myself into this? Why is everybody acting this way?

"You shouldn't have done that," Jessie said.

"Who, *me?*" Rockett demanded defensively. "What about all of you guys who can't even behave decently for, like, five minutes?"

"I was talking about Max," Jessie said softly, her pale face flushing with embarrassment.

"Behave decently? Get over yourself, Movado," Sharla protested. "You sound like my mother."

A shushing sound, like wind rushing through the auditorium, heralded Ms. Tinydahl's entrance. Suddenly, everyone was in their seats, all quiet and facing forward.

Except for Rockett, who was standing up on the stage, clutching her clipboard and feeling like an epic jerk.

I can't believe I just did what I so didn't want to do — get all bent and bossy, lose my temper and my sense of humor, embarrass my most supportive bud, and, like, publicly scold the boy I'm crushed on.

Ms. Tinydahl was watching her with furrowed brow. Had the English teacher overheard the fuss? Was she thinking what everyone else probably was, that Rockett Movado was the wrong girl for the job?

"Rockett," Ms. T greeted her as she mounted the stairs to the stage. "Are we ready, dear?"

As Rockett passed her the clipboard, Mr. Baldus entered the auditorium.

"Let the games begin!" he shouted. "That's how the Roman emperors signaled the start of competition in the Colosseum. All set?" he asked Rockett, taking the stage steps two at a time.

"The schedule looks good." Ms. Tinydahl gave Rockett a stopwatch and showed her how to use it. "Can you time the acts? Each should be no longer than five minutes."

"Less is even better," Mr. Baldus counseled.

"We can work on streamlining them later. Attention, class," Ms. Tinydahl called. "This is excellent. Seventeen of you have signed up to audition. Because of time constraints, I must remind you that only ten acts will actually perform in the show. The rest of you will see Rockett to volunteer for or be assigned other important functions. All right now. Arnold," Ms. Tinydahl called, checking the list, then returning the board to Rockett.

Whitney's hand shot up.

"Um, there's a minor issue," Rockett explained. "Whitney and Nicole would like to go before Arnold —"

"Totally not," Nicole protested, signaling Whitney to

44

lower her hand. "We wouldn't think of upsetting the schedule. I mean, so what that Rockett practically ruined our act by getting one of its most important participants to drop out? Whitney and I are completely supportive of this talent show, and we will so go forward in an orderly sportswomanlike manner."

Feeling herself begin to blush, Rockett climbed off the stage as Arnold clambered up.

"I'm sorry I snapped at you," she whispered to Jessie.

"That must have been so hard, standing up there getting dissed," her friend commiserated. "I thought Max acted like a major Moe."

"Ready?" Ms. Tinydahl said. "Rockett, up here, please." She patted the stool next to hers. "You'll be here, next to me."

"A reminder, talent tikes," Mr. Baldus called out. "We're looking for a combo of originality, real talent, and tight timing."

Rockett hurried back onto the stage and, at Ms. T's signal, started the stopwatch.

Arnold was shuffling a thick deck of cards. "This'll work a lot better when I have an assistant," he assured the teachers.

Holding the deck with two fingers, he reached inside his shirt for something. A flow of colored scarves erupted from his sleeve. "I need someone to hand me stuff," he explained.

Suddenly, the cards shot from his fingers, fanning out at high speed into the front rows.

Jessie, Arrow, and Viva covered their faces with their hands. Kids were scrambling out of the way of the fractured deck.

"Uh-oh, duck!" someone shouted as a white bird wriggled free of Arnold's pocket and sped frantic and low over the auditorium.

"It needs a little work, I know," the hapless magician confided. "Can I try it again when I have my assistant?"

Mr. Baldus and Ms. Tinydahl were staring at him, stunned. "There's an opening at five tomorrow," Rockett told them.

"All righty, then," Mr. Baldus agreed.

"Next!" Ms. Tinydahl called after the gawky boy had gathered up his fallen scarves and the few cards still onstage.

"I knew I could count on you," Arnold whispered to Rockett as Nicole and Whitney bounded up the stairs. "Now all I need is a partner. I'll be counting on your help with that problem, too!"

"We haven't got our music set yet, so this'll be a little rough, okay?" Whitney was saying to Ms. Tinydahl.

"And, like, you've got to imagine a third girl here," Nicole announced. "Stephanie just dropped out. Thanks to our meddling stage manager."

The cheerleading duet was energetic. They tumbled and jumped, did splits, somersaults, back flips, and strange lopsided arrangements.

"You'd think they would have adjusted things just a little," Arnold, who was still onstage standing in the wings, remarked. "I mean, you can tell they're trying to do a pyramid but it doesn't work with just the two of them."

"They're running long, too," Rockett confided.

With an energetic cry, Nicole threw herself into Whitney's outstretched arms. With help, Whitney might have caught her. Instead, as Whitney's arms faltered, Nicole grabbed her bud's shoulders for balance, tugging her forward into a headfirst roll that collapsed over Nicole's falling body like a tidal wave.

"Yard sale!" Sharla hollered at the sight of them wiped out, their crushed pom-poms sprawled across the stage.

"How'd we do?" Nicole asked enthusiastically as soon as she was on her feet again.

"It seemed a little . . . rough, dear," Ms. Tinydahl said delicately, "and long." She looked at Rockett for confirmation.

"Well?" Nicole asked, hands on hips.

Rockett nodded. "You went over," she said softly, not wanting to deliver the bad news so loudly that everyone heard.

"Could you mumble more? Hello, I am so not skilled at lipreading!" Nicole announced.

"You went over a little," Rockett repeated louder.

"A little?" Dana laughed. "They went over like a ton of bricks!"

"I told you it wasn't going to work without Steph." Whitney got up, brushing off her lace-lined hot-pink cheerleading skirt. "We should have redone our stunts."

"You redo them," Nicole snapped. "I am so over this weak idea. Ms. Tinydahl, Mr. Baldus, I'd like to try out again tomorrow. Alone. I've got this moving reading I'd like to give. It's from an amazing self-help book Reginald, my father, recommended — *Negotiating Kindergarten to Win*. I think everyone here could so benefit from it. Shall we say three-thirty tomorrow?"

Rockett checked her list and shook her head. "That's taken. Four-twenty is available."

"Whatever," Nicole said, starting down the steps.

Whitney followed her forlornly. "But, Nic, what about me?"

"Don't you see, this is fate." Arnold rushed after them. "I think I've got a spot for you in my act," he said, trying to sound casual.

"Yeeeech!" Whitney replied, storming off.

Hmmm. Rockett flipped through the sheets on her clipboard until she found the torn picture of the costume Arnold wanted for his assistant. *Actually, Whitney would look brutally choice in this outfit. She'd make the coolest magician's assistant ever. She's out of an act now. It would be perfect — except for the fact that she thinks Arnold is the geek of the universe.*

"Who's next?" Mr. Baldus wanted to know. Rockett checked her pad. "The 'Delta Girls Blues' project," she announced.

Darnetta, Jessie, and Viva scrambled onto the stage. "We've been practicing with this record of my mom's, but

Rockett's gonna get us the real music soon," Darnetta explained.

Then, snapping her fingers, she launched into a gravelly voiced blues number. After two false starts, Jessie got behind her on the flute. And then Viva slinked in from the wings, twisting and moving and looking professionally jazzy, Rockett thought.

The act won applause and cheers. "Very nice, girls," Ms. Tinydahl said. She glanced at Rockett, who checked the stopwatch and nodded. "Your timing was fine. Well in under the whistle. Thank you, girls."

As Darnetta led her ecstatic troupe off the stage, Rockett said, "They were great, weren't they?"

"The performance was lovely." Ms. Tinydahl smiled. "But I'm afraid Viva's costume won't do," she added softly.

"Um, won't do what?" Rockett asked.

Sharla was standing near the stage. "The Tiny-doll's nixing the stretchy bodysuit, bet?" she murmured.

"You mean you don't like Viva's leotard?" Rockett asked Ms. Tinydahl.

"I'm sure she can find something more appropriate," the teacher said. "Tell her as tactfully as you can."

Wow, I so disagree, Rockett thought. *I love that outfit. And so does Viva. It totally makes the act. Viva's gonna be so hurt. Ms. Tinydahl can't expect me to break the news to her. I feel like such a stooge.*

"Who's next?" Ms. Tinydahl asked.

Stephanie stood. "That would be me. Only I didn't bring my parrot, Ms. T."

"Stephanie, you wanted the last slot available," Rockett objected. "I've got you down for Saturday."

"Get flexible," Stephanie said crossly. "Anyway, I'm not actually auditioning. I thought I'd just describe my act. Mr. Baldus said you wanted originality. Well, Ms. Tinydahl, I'm going to do this fabulous bird thingy with Panama. It'll be a total first. He's my parrot, and he can say, 'Way,' 'I don't think so,' and 'Not even.' Isn't that brilliant?"

"Like what's the act?" Dana demanded.

Stephanie stopped, then said, "Ask Rockett. It was all her idea. My best buds are all bent out of shape 'cause I bowed out of their act. And now nobody likes my parrot act, either? That is so typical. Well, thank you very much, Rockett."

"Um, we'll work something out," Rockett promised, too embarrassed to look at the teachers. "I've still got you penciled in to audition tomorrow. I'll come up with something."

"Rosales," Mr. Baldus called. "You're up."

Ruben scrambled onstage with his guitar. "Are these the amps?" he asked Rockett.

"Um, they're what Mr. Baldus brought up from the band room," she fudged.

"Not the ones I'm gonna trash, right?"

"I didn't know you needed them for the audition —"

Ruben laughed. "I wasn't going to blow them now. Okay, I'll just plug in and play a few riffs and, like, explain the finale," he said, fiddling with the big boxy amplifiers.

"What does he mean, he's not going to blow them now, dear?" Ms. Tinydahl leaned over and asked Rockett. "What does he intend to blow?"

"A set of amps," Rockett said as Ruben lit into his solo.

The noise was fierce. Rockett and Ms. Tinydahl, and even some of the kids in the audience, held their ears. Mr. Baldus just snapped his fingers, his eyes closed ecstatically.

"Now this is where I start really revving," Ruben roared after a while. "And I'm burnin' up the clouds. The old guitar is squealing and screeching. And then, right about here, I take it up a notch and *kahblooey*! Sparks will fly."

"I think not," Ms. Tinydahl said at the final chord. She gave Mr. Baldus a knowing look.

"Well, not these," Ruben explained. "These belong to the school. I know that. But Rockett's gonna find me some used amps to fry."

"And you intend to ratchet the music to such a deafening volume that the amplifiers will . . . er, explode?" Ms. Tinydahl asked.

Explode? Yes, that was what he'd said. He was going to destroy the amps. Explode them. Rockett felt sick just thinking about it. How could she have been so dense? He'd only said it, like, a hundred times.

"Um, yup. That's the plan," Ruben informed them. "Didn't the *stage manager* let you in on it?"

"*Baaaap!* Cannot be done," Mr. Baldus said, like a quiz master signaling a wrong answer.

"If Rockett had informed us, I'd have squelched the idea that much sooner," Ms. Tinydahl said with unusual firmness. "I'm sorry, Ruben. I will not risk damaging the school electrical system and, even more to the point, risk our audience's well-being. And, I believe, Ruben, that your solo ran overlong."

"No way!" The upset boy glared at Rockett. "That wasn't even the whole thing. I was just giving you guys a little taste. She can't be right."

"You went over, Ruben," Rockett said resolutely. She was angry at herself for being such a bonehead. But she was also bugged at Ruben for coming up with such a whack scheme. "Like about two minutes."

"Well, that totally tears it." Ruben yanked his guitar cords out of the speakers. "I thought you were on my side," he grumbled at Rockett and thundered down the stairs.

"Cleveland and Max," Ms. Tinydahl called, "our comedy team."

"Send in the clowns!" Mr. Baldus shouted. "That's the name of a song," he explained.

A few kids laughed politely at his limp quip. Cleve and Max did only slightly better. Five out of their twenty-eight tired jokes drew giggles. The rest went down like the *Titanic*.

"That was embarrassingly awful," Dana announced as the wanna-be comics wound down their audition.

"They weren't that bad," Whitney loyally protested. "I mean, I liked the one about the guy rushing into the doctor's office, saying, 'I think I'm shrinking.'"

"And the doctor says, 'You'll have to be *a little patient.*' Yeah, that was cute," Stephanie said on behalf of her boy buds.

"Hey, wait," Max hollered. "We've got a bunch of bumper-sticker jokes, too!"

"Yeah," said Cleve. "Like, there's one that goes, If at First You Don't Succeed, Skydiving's Not for You."

Sharla Rae cracked up. "Why didn't you think of that before?" she challenged.

"And here's one for science buffs," Max offered. "Gravity . . . It's Not Just a Good Idea. It's the Law."

Mr. Baldus led the laughter.

"How about: Old Age Comes at a Bad Time?" Cleve called out desperately.

"Too little, too late," Dana decreed, laughing.

Ms. Tinydahl smiled demurely. "I'm afraid we're out of time," she said. "Thank you all."

Some kids stood and stretched. Others slapped five. A small group of supporters surrounded Ruben. A few rushed to console Max and Cleve. Most began to file out of the auditorium. Some were murmuring excitedly. But others were grumbling.

Rockett sat onstage, staring at her clipboard. She'd acted like a jerk before tryouts even started, standing up onstage like a kindergarten teacher trying to get kids to stop squirting and throwing stuff. She'd snapped at Arnold for laughing at her. And at Jessie, by mistake. She'd tried to help Stephanie and wound up getting Whitney cut from the show. Plus parrot girl had not only jumped the audition lineup, but done a 360 from gratitude to blame. . . .

"Buck up, dear," Ms. Tinydahl urged. "Not everyone's going to be pleased with audition results. That's why we, the faculty, make the difficult decisions. But you will speak to Viva, won't you?"

"Yes," Rockett said. "But Ms. Tinydahl, I, um . . . I think you're wrong about that costume —"

"And about Ruben's solo, too, I suppose."

"No," she said after a moment, "not about that."

"You did a good job today," Ms. Tinydahl assured her, then left the auditorium.

Before Rockett hit the bottom step, she was surrounded by kids.

"You see how badly I need an assistant," Arnold said.

"Maybe what you need is a new act." Rockett felt tired suddenly and cranky.

"I'm the one who needs a new act," Whitney murmured sadly. "Thanks to you, Rockett. Why did you have to talk Stephanie into that dumb parrot act?"

"Which is so not going to work," Stephanie com-

54

plained. "Not unless you figure out what I'm supposed to do."

"I thought you were on my side," Ruben snapped at her. He was standing with Wolf, who was watching her, too, waiting for her response.

"I am," Rockett said, frustrated. No way was she gonna tell him that she agreed with Ms. Tinydahl about the amplifiers. Nor that she felt like the ultimate dork for not understanding that he'd planned to blow up electrical equipment onstage. "It's just that your solo was too long."

"Well, it's gonna be a lot shorter when I don't do it at all," Ruben raged. "So much for artistic freedom. Let's blow this joint," he said to Wolf.

"Poor word choice, *amigo*." Wolf grinned, then they stomped up the aisle.

With a strange, brimming sadness, Rockett watched them go. She couldn't believe any of this was happening — but she was beginning to understand why this job had made Nicole even worse than usual.

"We're in, right?" Darnetta, Viva, and Jessie circled her suddenly, blocking her view of Ruben.

She pulled herself together. "You guys were so great," she said.

"But?" Darnetta read her expression.

"Was Sharla right? Is it my costume?" Viva asked, all worried.

"Ms. Tinydahl thinks it's inappropriate," Rockett forced herself to say.

Viva slumped. "Oh, beans! What am I gonna do now? This outfit just *makes* my routine."

"Rockett, you've got to do something," Jessie urged.

"Yeah, talk to Ms. T," Darnetta demanded. "Make her change her mind."

Arrow appeared and put her arm around Viva's shoulder. "Rockett's one of the good guys, Viva. Trust her. She'll fix it," she predicted. "Rockett, have you gotten a chance to talk to Lutzi yet about my target?"

"Um, no, not yet," she said, grateful for the vote of confidence. She really liked Arrow. The girl had so much going for her, including a choice combo of self-assurance and generosity. "You know, I've been thinking about your act," Rockett began, then stopped and looked around.

She *had* been thinking about it — and an archery demonstration wasn't all that golden a notion. Kind of dull, actually. Plus, Ms. Tinydahl wasn't gonna be much happier having someone shooting arrows in the auditorium than she was about Ruben blowing up amps.

But this was definitely not the time or place to share her concerns with Arrow. There were too many other kids around.

"It's a neat idea, right?" Arrow pressed.

"Um . . ." Rockett hedged as the smiling girl waited for her answer. Darnetta, Jessie, and Viva were waiting, too. "S'cool," she finally murmured.

"Fully," Arrow affirmed, leading her downcast friend away.

"We're depending on you," Darnetta insisted, following Arrow and Viva.

Right, Darnetta. And if you hadn't taken the job I wanted, you'd be complaining to someone else right now. Like maybe yourself!

"Are you okay?" Jessie asked when they'd gone.

From her first-row seat, Nicole was watching them.

"Sure," Rockett said, trying to sound cheerful.

"You look kinda stressed," her worried bud insisted.

"Hey, I'm fine." She wished Jessie would just forget it. The tough-love leader of The Ones was taking in every word.

"Maybe you could tell Tinydahl that you need some help —"

"No," Rockett snapped, aware of Nicole's smirking gaze. "I'm okay, Jessie. I don't need help."

"Well, I would. I'd go see her and —"

"Cut it out," Rocket hissed.

"Gee, maybe you should." Nicole stood abruptly, brushed off her skirt, and turned to Rockett, her face all puckered with bogus concern. "It's a little early in the game to run crying for help," she said, strolling past them to the exit, "but you do look like you're so hurtin'."

Did Jessie have to talk about me needing help in front of Ni-cold-heart? Ugh, so embarrassing. I wish I'd just told everyone how I really feel. Like Arrow's archery idea? Snooze alert. But I don't want to hurt Arrow's feelings — she's been totally sensitive to mine.

If I tell everyone the truth, no one will like me. If I just keep on being supportive, I'll go down in Whistling Pines history as the lamest stage manager ever.

But maybe there's another choice here? Like . . . what Jessie said, asking for help.

Confession Session

Rockett's hangin' in better than I thought she would. Maybe Jessie's right about the girl — that she's really cool and all. We'll see . . . when she convinces Ms. T that Viva's costume is the bomb.

I'm glad my crew split up for the talent show. And I wonder if my soul mate, Wolf, will like my act as much as Rockett does? That would be sooo excellent.

How superficially do I care that everyone's all drooling to be in the talent show. I don't need a stage to flaunt my mega-gifts. But it would be neat to search my fave secondhand shops for costumes and props. I know precisely right where Arnold clot-brain's glittering assistant's gown is hangin'. And how to find tons of moldy sheet music.

CHAPTER SIX

"Well, are you going in or not?" Hands on her hips, Jessie was all up in Rockett's face. They were standing in front of Ms. Tinydahl's room.

"Give me a break, Jessie. I'm still thinking," Rockett urged.

"Well, I wish you'd thought *twice* before dissing me in front of Nicole," her bruised bud said.

"I'm sorry. I said I was sorry. I just didn't want her thinking I couldn't handle things. It's only the first day of auditions. I'm supposed to be putting together a whole show and I'm already a nervous wreck."

"Last year, Nicole was, too," Jessie pointed out.

"Yeah, but she didn't go running to Ms. Tinydahl for help."

"Exactly," her best friend said.

Rockett smiled. "I see what you mean. Okay, then. Yuck. Here goes."

Ms. Tinydahl was at her desk when Rockett peeked in and rapped on the doorjamb.

"Oh, good," the teacher said, as if she'd been expecting her. "Come in."

Jessie gave Rockett a little push, then waited outside.

61

"Um, Ms. Tinydahl . . . I'm, uh . . . The reason I came to see you is . . ."

"Is it about the show, dear?"

Rockett nodded.

"You're having a difficult time?" the teacher asked.

"Kind of," Rockett conceded.

"I know, dear. Our stage managers usually do. Which is not to say that you're not doing a good job." Ms. Tinydahl put down her pen and gave Rockett her full attention. "Don't confuse the two."

"Uh, thanks," she said. "I just need . . . I mean, I think I'd like —"

"A little help, is that it?"

"I guess," Rockett confessed. Ms. Tinydahl's vibes were better than Mavis's. Rockett was grateful for her mind-reading skills.

"I thought you might." Ms. T smiled kindly. "Which is why I've taken the liberty of asking Mr. Zeitbaum to work with you."

"Arnold?!" Rockett gasped.

"I noticed that he'd expressed an interest in the job. I'm sure he'll be helpful," Ms. Tinydahl was saying, without realizing that Rockett's life — at least the near-future portion of it — was flashing before her eyes and it was so not a pretty sight. "I can tell you that he's very excited about it. I spoke with him not five minutes ago."

"You already talked to him?" The part where everyone knew she was a loser was becoming more vivid.

"He's highly motivated and thrilled to have been asked. He's going to be a great help to you," Ms. Tinydahl declared in a voice that let Rockett know the subject was closed. "Actually," she added, "I think our first round of auditions went fairly well. Is there anything else, dear?"

Anything else? Down, verging on desperate, Rockett wanted to crawl out of the room before Ms. T. had any more brilliant ideas. But there were other issues that needed airing. With or without Arnold's so-called assistance, she was still stage manager and had stuff to say.

"Two things." She cleared her throat. "I agree with you that Ruben's finale won't work in a school auditorium, but everyone loves his sound. So I'm thinking maybe if he shortens his solo a little and, you know, blows off the sparky ending, that he should be in the show."

"Well, I'll consider it," Ms. Tinydahl offered.

"And then there's Viva's costume —"

"It's just too much," the teacher decreed.

"But it totally works with the way Darnetta sings that song and Jessie's kinda sad, jazzy flute."

"Viva's dancing was wonderful. The costume, however . . ." She shook her head. "I'm afraid not."

"But Viva loves it. She got it especially for the talent show."

"Rockett, you're bright, creative, imaginative. All wonderful leadership qualities. I suggest you put some of that imagination to work on this problem and come to me with a solution, one that will work for both Viva and the faculty."

Rockett mumbled something and left the room before Ms. T could go any further.

Jessie was waiting. "So what did she say?"

"You so don't want to know," Rockett assured her, opting for denial. But, as usual, Arnold hung out where he wasn't wanted, loitering annoyingly in her thoughts.

Jessie was quiet for a second, then she said, "I do want to know."

"Two words. Arnold Zeitbaum," Rockett said.

Jessie gasped.

"Any other bright ideas?"

"Did someone just mention the Moron of Zoron or am I only waking from a frightmare?"

Mavis had obviously overheard them talking about Arnold. "I knew I'd find you here, Rockett," she continued. "My brain waves were tingling like crazy all the whole way down the hall just now."

"Hey, guys." Arrow joined them. "I've got gym next period, Rockett, and I was just wondering whether . . . ?" With a sheepish laugh, she let it drop. "Boy, I'm turning into a big-time pest, right?"

"Did I ask Ms. Lutzi about your target?" Rockett guessed. "Not yet." One, she hadn't had time to; two, she wished Arrow would change her mind. . . .

"Ugh, I'm like totally obsessing about my act," Arrow confessed. "I don't know what I'll do if Lutzi says no."

"Well, I'd like to talk to you about it," Rockett said.

"Shoot." Arrow laughed. "Shoot? See, I told you I was obsessing. This is as good a time as any."

"Not exactly." Rockett glanced at Mavis.

"I know exactly right where to find an excellent bull's-eye-type target for which Arrow could practice with," Mavis piped up. "There's this junk shop that's got old sports equipment by the gazillions."

"Excellent," Arrow said. "Go on, Rockett. What did you want to tell me?"

Rockett glanced at Jessie and Mavis. Both of them were looking at her expectantly. Arrow was smiling, waiting.

"Well, uh," she began. "Actually, Arrow, I don't think Ms. Tinydahl's going to go for the bow-and-arrow thing. It's kind of like a safety hazard. And, well, even if it wasn't, I think the idea is not really all that, like . . . theatrical."

"You think it's boring?"

"I didn't say that," Rockett protested.

"No," Arrow snapped. "What you *did* say was you thought it was a cool idea. Rockett, I'm slated to audition for the talent show tomorrow — and now you're saying basically my act bites. Thanks for your help."

"I'm sure she doesn't mean —" Jessie tried to help.

Rockett was racing through the file bins in her brain, trying to remember the list of talents Arrow's buds had rattled off. What besides archery rocked the multigifted girl?

She's a drum-banging, in-line-skating, guitar-strumming, songwriting, keyboard-slammin', soul-singing, volleyball-playing archery buff, Viva had recited.

Drum banging. Who else had mentioned drum banging?

Wolf! Rockett remembered. *The boy Arrow was crushed out on. And he wasn't participating in the show yet. It'd be so hot if they teamed up.*

Brainstorm!

"Arrow, wait. Listen. How about Wolf?"

The girl perked up at the mention of his name. "What about Wolf?"

"Well, maybe instead of archery, you two could get together and do, like, a drumming thing."

At that, Arrow's dark eyes sparkled.

"That would really blow kids away," Rockett went on, encouraged. "You know, like drumming, dancing, maybe some Native American songs or chants or whatever . . ."

"You are onto somethin'. But I'm not sure Wolf would catch the fever," Arrow said.

"Oh, he so would," Rockett insisted.

"You think so?" Jessie sounded doubtful.

"My tingling scalp tells me, Rockett, that you are off the Wolf track." Suddenly, Mavis was in the mix. "Wolf is not your basic joiner who trots with the pack. Like my own very self, he does not seek the spotlight."

"She's right," Arrow admitted with regret.

"No way," Rockett insisted. "I mean, he practically told me how much he'd love to do it."

She was going a little overboard, she knew. But she

66

had to give Arrow some hope, didn't she? Plus, even if Wolf hadn't totally said he wanted to be in the show, it was still a great idea. He'd want to be in it once he knew about it.

"He did? What did he say?" Jessie wanted to know.

Why wasn't Jessie getting it? Couldn't she see how psyched Arrow was and how neat it would be to pair her with Wolf for the talent show?

"You remember," Rockett prompted her, "like when we were talking about the show and Wolf brought up that powwow he'd been to and the drumming and all."

"He said he'd love to drum for the show?" Arrow asked.

"I think that was it. Right, Jessie?"

"Not exactly." Jessie was frowning big-time.

"I knew you'd be a great stage manager!" Arrow leaped at Rockett and hugged her wildly. "Thanks. I can't wait to catch up with Wolf."

"What was that about?" Jessie asked as Arrow hurried down the hall.

"That's what I'd like to know," Rockett grumbled. "Couldn't you have helped me out a little?"

"Helped you lie to Arrow, you mean?"

"Oh, come on, Jess. It wasn't a lie. Wolf did say he'd drummed at a powwow, right? And Arrow really needs a new act. Ms. Tinydahl would've definitely vetoed the bow-and-arrow number, and Ms. Lutzi would never have lent us a gym target —"

Mavis cleared her throat loudly. "I know where a target can be found and possibly even might be maybe donated for school purposes. And it happens to be right practically around the corner from the vintage music store that has multiple stacks of, like, all old jazz —"

"Mavis, are you volunteering to do props?" Rockett asked gratefully.

"Well, I do most certainly know better than anyone where to find excellent, fun used goods," the psychic girl asserted.

"Ah, maidens fair and foul! That's you, Wartella breath, on the foul end of my greeting." Arnold jogged up to them, grinning gleefully. "A grammatical correction. The words *props* and *Mavis* do not — repeat, *do not* — belong on the same page. If ever there was a person nonproper it's you, oh frizz-headed harridan of Depew-ville. Hey, did you hear, Rockett, I'm your new assistant stage manager!"

"Ms. Tinydahl just told me," she confessed glumly.

"I am instantly withdrawing my offer right now!" Mavis snapped, and stormed away, nearly bumping into Ruben, who was heading their way.

"Oh, great, Arnold," Rockett let loose. "You just lost us a prop person. That's why I didn't want you as a helper!"

The sci-fi nerd, usually way overconfident and never at a lost for words, gaped at her.

"Rockett, don't," Jessie cautioned her.

"Why not?" She turned on her friend. "I'm trying as hard as I can, Jessie. But no matter what I do, some people — including my close personals — find something to gripe about or blame me for. I took your advice. I asked for help. And look what I got. *Arnold!*"

Ruben was moving past them, head down, hands in the pockets of his baggies, looking grumpy. "News flash," he barked, without slowing down, "Stage Manager Throws a Hissy Fit. Whoops, I forgot. That's not news. It's déjà vu all over again."

"What did he mean by that?" Rockett whimpered.

"I guess he means you're acting like Nicole," Jessie answered.

Is it true? Or are Ruben and Jessie all sour grapes because of their own issues?

If I were seriously mimicking the queen of mean, would I have asked for help? But no, I listened to my so-called main bud, Jessie, and what did I get? Arnold!!! And the first thing Grandmaster Geek does is cost me a prop person.

So I lost it. . . . Ugh. But everyone's allowed, like, one diva moment, right? It just feels like every decision I made was the wrong one. Well, here comes one that's gotta work: I am so going home and crashing. At least I can count on privacy and downtime there.

Confession Session

Okay, my feelings were bruised when Rockett admitted she didn't think my archery idea had much pizzazz. But I give the girl credit for telling me the truth. More, for not just taking me down, but coming up with an excellent alternative!

What is happening here? Honesty is the most important thing there is between friends — and now Rockett's mad at me for being truthful?

CHAPTER SEVEN

The battered, old car in the driveway was her first clue. The laundry bag in the hall was the second.

Rockett hoped against hope that she was wrong about these telltale signs. But then she opened the door to her very own room — the solitary sanctuary of peace and downtime she'd been longing for — and saw her big sister stretched out on the guest bed.

"Juno," she groaned. "What are you doing here?"

She was on the phone, Rockett's phone. "Um, excuse me." Juno clamped her hand over the receiver. "Hey, Rock," she said, all smiley-faced and relaxed. "What's up? You look kind of stressed. Give me a minute, I'll be right off, okay?"

Rockett did a 180, her heels squeaking on the floor. "Mom," she called, racing to the kitchen. "Mom! What is going on?"

The smell of something delicious baking in the oven told her that her mother had been there, although she wasn't now. The dirty milk glass in the sink and the plate of cookie crumbs left on the table clued her that Juno had also come and gone . . . into Rockett's shelter, her haven, her room.

Oh, no, not again. The last time Juno showed up, Mom

and Dad at least asked my permission for her to bunk in with me. And I said yes because Dad was working on a new invention and had his equipment all over Juno's space. This time no one bothered to ask me at all.

"Hey, Rockett. Are you okay?" Her sister had followed her into the kitchen. She was looking all concerned now. Her face scrunched with compassion. "Are you bugged at me or something?"

Rockett flopped down into a chair. "No," she said. "You were right the first time. I'm just stressed. And totally surprised to see you. What are you doing home?"

Juno had been sick, last time. Worn down from working too hard at school. But she looked totally healthy now.

"Oh, I miss you guys, you know. Anyway, no classes tomorrow, so I just took off for a long, luxurious weekend —"

"— in my room?" Rockett said.

"Is it okay? Dad's all set up in mine again. I didn't think you'd mind. Should've asked, I guess. So what's stressing you?"

"Nothing. I mean, I volunteered to be stage manager for the class talent show —"

"You go, girl!" As always, her sister was fully supportive.

"Yeah, well, thanks. It's nothing. Nothing I can't handle."

The wall phone rang before Juno could quiz her further. Rockett jumped for it, but Juno was closer.

72

College girl picked it up, then quickly winced and held it away from her ear. "I think you want my sister. Hang on," she said, handing Rockett the phone. "Must be for you."

"You said he said he wanted to do it!" a peeved voice, which Rockett immediately recognized as Arrow's, accused.

"Excuse me. Slow down." Rockett glanced at Juno, who was just standing there watching her, listening to every word. "I can't really get into it right now, Arrow, but trust me, okay? Whoops, can you hang on? There's my call waiting."

She clicked in the other call.

"You gotta convince Tinydahl to let me do my solo. I'll cut it and all, but I gotta keep that rockin' ending —"

"I'm on the other line, Ruben, can I get back to you?" she asked, wondering whatever happened to her plan to just chill — then remembering: Juno happened. Then the phone happened.

"I'll hold," Ruben decided.

"Arrow," she got back on with the distressed girl. "Listen, it'll all work out. We'll talk, I promise, okay?" She wished her sister would quit staring at her. "Or better still, for *privacy*," she emphasized, "e-mail me."

She clicked off with Arrow, and Ruben was back on the line.

"Ruben, that ending . . . It's . . . I can't really talk right now. Okay, e-mail me in five minutes and we'll work it out, okay?"

"Problems?" Juno asked.

"Not even," Rockett said, hanging up. "Just, you know, challenges."

"Oh, gosh. E-mail. You need your computer, right? I was just using it. I hope you don't mind. I've gotta turn in a project on Monday. It'll just take me a minute to save what I was working on, okay?" Juno threw her an apologetic smile and hurried out of the kitchen.

"Sure," Rockett murmured.

This is so not what I need right now: Ms. I-can-do-every-thing-and-stay-totally-cool invading my room and my life. I mean, look at her. She's under pressure, she's got a tight dead-line, and she's all like ho-hum, going, 'So, well, what's up, little sis? You look stressed.' It just makes me feel so pathetic.

Rockett sank into a chair at the table. She was aimlessly mashing the cookie crumbs on Juno's plate when the telephone rang again. The sound startled her. She jumped up automatically and reached for the wall phone, then hesitated. She'd come home to crash and burn, not take a ton of calls.

"It's for you!" Juno shouted from the bedroom. "Rockett, pick up."

Great. Now she had no choice. Whoever was on the line knew she was home. Thanks to her helpful big sister.

It was Whitney. "Listen, Rockett, I'm not blaming you — exactly" was how the girl opened the conversation. "But I do think you owe me."

"Owe you what?" Rockett asked, trying to sound upbeat and polite. It wasn't Whitney's fault she was irked at Juno.

"Well, an act, for starters. Nic's gonna read her self-help book and Stephanie's all Dr. Doolittle. But I am odd-girl-out, utterly without a clue about what to do for the talent show."

Rockett could totally relate. "Believe me, Whitney, I know how you feel," she tried to comfort the bummed One. "I was so there myself just a few days ago —"

"Oh, but now you're stage manager. You don't have time for the 'little people' anymore? What is that whack noise?! Are you getting another call?"

"Um, sounds like it," Rockett said. "Can you hold for a sec?" She clicked call waiting again.

"I was just trying to save you from the wily Wartella worm when you turned on me most foully," Arnold announced. "But I've decided to give you another chance."

"Arnold, Mavis was volunteering for a chore I so need help with, and you totally blew her off."

"Let's not quibble and squabble —"

"I can't get into it now. I've got Whitney on the other line."

"Whitney?! I can't believe it." Arnold's voice rose to a frantic shriek. "This is fate, don't you see. It's kismet, karma, written in the stars —"

"You're sounding like Mavis," Rockett couldn't help commenting.

"If you mean drastically desperate, you're right. I must have fair Whitney in my act."

"Hold that thought," Rockett ordered, getting back to Whitney. "Whitney, I want to help you. I really do. And I will, I just need a little time to focus on the problem —"

"There's just not that much time left, Rockett. I'm frantic."

Arnold wants Whitney. Whitney wants an act. But can I just come right out and suggest they merge? Nu-uh. Whitney's radically anti-Arnold. Which is so too bad because she'd look great in that glittery gold costume.

"Well, um," Rockett said, wracking her brain for a way to drop a hint, bring up the subject, just kinda *mention* the possibility, "what are you good at?"

"What do you mean, like buying clothes, planning parties? I'm excellent at that stuff. Plus I can be deeply diplomatic, you know, like very tactful. I'm seriously social —"

"And you, um, you look amazing in clothes, right?"

"Yes, that's something else I'm good at."

"Well, er, how frantic are you?" Rockett asked cautiously.

"What do you mean?" Whitney responded.

"Whitney, have you even seen the costume Arnold has in mind for his assistant?"

"Arnold, that bozo, that nauseating nerd?! Are you suggesting I do a duet with Repulso the Geekboy?"

"Well, um, it was just a thought because, honestly, Whitney, the magician's assistant's outfit — which Mavis says she can definitely get us — is fantastic. . . ."

With a loud "Yeech!!" Whitney hung up.

"What'd she say?" Arnold asked. "I wanna know."

"Believe me, Arnold, you so don't. And anyway, I don't think I could reproduce the sound. Hold on."

Suddenly, Juno was back in the kitchen. Rockett put her hand over the receiver. "Yes?" she said to her sister.

"Your computer's free now. Are you gonna be on the phone long? I'm sorry, Rock. It's just that I'm expecting a call."

"Arnold, I've gotta go —"

"No, no, no." Juno waved at her. "No, don't get off. That isn't what I mean. I was just asking —"

Rockett hung up, relieved to be rid of the desperate boy. Then she faced Juno, sighing deeply, as if she'd done her this tremendous favor by getting off the phone.

Juno walked past her to the stove. "Mom's meeting Dad after work," she said, grabbing the pot holders and peering into the hot, delicious-smelling oven. "She was gonna leave you a note but I said I'd tell you. They're going to check out an art show tonight. So I made a lasagna, just for us."

Oh, no, not another charitable act of niceness!

"Thanks, Juno." Rockett's shoulders sunk into loser mode.

By the time she got back to her room and checked her e-mail, there were messages waiting from Ruben and Arrow.

Talk about a choice. It was like who did she want to dump on her first?

She hit Quit, opting for time, and the phone rang again. This time she and Juno answered it in different rooms at the same time.

A boy's voice said, "Hello?"

Juno went, "Josh?"

Josh?

The boy said, "Um, Rockett?"

Rockett said, "I'm on, Juno."

Juno said, "Oh, I'm sorry. I thought it was for me."

There was a pause when no one spoke, and then everyone spoke at once.

"Okay, well, I'm hanging up," Juno said, and did.

"Who was that?" Wolf asked.

"My sister. Hi, Wolf, wussup?" Rockett said.

Finally, the conversation got into gear. "Wussup?" Wolf echoed. "That's what I'd like to know. Arrow said you said I said I wanted to do something with her for the talent show. What's that about?"

"It was just this gigundo misunderstanding, that's all," Rockett began backpedaling. "A basic communications blooper, you know."

"No, I don't know. What do you mean?" Wolf was leaving her no wiggle room.

"Well, um, actually, Wolf, I was thinking, like, what are you gonna do for the show? Mr. Baldus says everyone has to participate —"

"I'll sign on with the sound crew, I guess. If my man Ruben wasn't set on soloing, I'd have maybe backed him on tambourine . . . or drum. It was amazin' banging that

78

old Pawnee hand drum my grandpop gave me. Man, you know, till I mentioned it to you the other day, I hadn't thought about that powwow in a long time," Wolf said.

Rockett's brain, which had been frozen in the I-am-so-busted position, started cranking.

"But Ruben does want to go solo this year, right?" she said. "So that won't work. But how about if . . . I mean, what I was thinking — which is what I guess I might have, like, just happened to *mention* to Arrow — was that you two should maybe consider doing some of that, you know, drumming and dancing and all. Together."

"Is that what she was talking about?" Wolf asked. Then he fell silent.

Rockett felt like jumping in, filling the space with words, but something told her — her speeding brain, she guessed — that it would be so the wrong approach.

"I don't know," Wolf said after a while. "I mean, we're from two different nations."

"Is that, like, a big problem?" she asked cautiously.

Wolf was silent for a beat. "Could be," he said. "Anyway, it's not like playing with Ruben, is it?"

"No," Rockett admitted. "Nothing like that at all."

Call waiting clicked again. And Juno walked into the room.

"Aren't you gonna get that?" Wolf asked as Rockett shot her sister a bogus stress-free smile.

"I'm talking to you now," she told Wolf. *And who knows what new problem is at the other end of the line. Of course, it might be the guy Juno's waiting to hear from.*

"No, go on. Pick it up," Wolf urged. "I got to think about this anyway."

"Okay, hang on. I'll be right back." Rockett hit the call-waiting button. Juno watched her do it.

"How fabu is that costume, *really?*"

Her sister was leaning toward her slightly, looking eager, clearly wanting to know who the call was for. And whether it was "Josh" on the line.

"It's for me," Rockett told her. "Hi, Whitney."

"I am not the least bit interested in doing anything with Zeit-bites. I don't even want to mention his name. We'll just call him he-who-makes-me-shudder. But how tasty is the gown? Is it really, really to die for?"

"On you it would be," Rockett said.

"And Mavis is definitely going to get it?"

"Um, well —" she hedged, glancing at her sister again — flawless Juno, who'd probably never stretch the truth even a teensy bit because she didn't have to worry about who liked her. "Definitely," Rockett said, turning her back on Juno. "Mavis is our prop person, and she will so snag that excellent costume."

"I'll get back to you," Whitney promised, and hung up.

"Wolf? Hello, Wolf?" But the boy was off the line, too.

Rockett replaced the receiver and faced her computer screen, hand hovering over the sign-on icon. Arrow or Ruben? Whose e-mail would she read first?

She spun around suddenly. "You know what, Juno. I'm

beat. You can use my computer if you need it. I'm just not up to answering e-mail tonight."

"I can understand it. The phone hasn't stopped ringing since you got home."

"It's not exactly about popularity," she said, trying to hang on to her carefree expression or at least keep the strained smile from sliding off her face. "It's just part of this stage manager thing I got myself into."

"More than you bargained for?" Juno asked innocently.

Rockett was right there. Right on the edge of telling the truth, spilling her woes to the real answer girl. But she forced herself to stop.

"No way," she said. "I am so pumped for this job. I mean, you know how it is when everyone needs you. But, hey, who's this Josh guy? And when are we gonna eat?"

I wanted downtime and now I am so down . . . as in downcast, downhearted, down under a heap of problems. Plus half the kids I know are down on me!

Jessie's steamed at me for not telling the truth, the whole truth, and nothing but . . . So why did I do it again just now, tonight, with Whitney! I can't believe I told her Mavis was definitely on our team when — thanks to my new assistant, Motor Mouth — she is so not.

I need Mavis back on board, scouting props and snagging costumes. I need help — and I don't mean Arnold aid!

I wish I could talk to Juno. But she'd never get it. Her life is so neat. And mine is so majorly messy!

Confession Session

Me do a powwow duet with Arrow in front of the whole school? I don't think so. Except it would be kinda cool wearin' my grandpop's old Pawnee breastplate and carryin' a dance stick wrapped in fur, eagle feathers, and beads. We're Plains Indians. Arrow's people come from, like, Carolina and Oklahoma. I wonder if she knows the grass dance, the crow hop, the sneak-up?

What does a magician's assistant do, anyway? I wouldn't have to actually talk to Arnold. I'd just be onstage looking fresh and, like, maybe hand him things. I wouldn't even have to look at him. Nicole and Steph would gag at the notion. But they blew me off in my hour of need. And I still want to be part of the show. I mean, what's my choice — painting scenery?

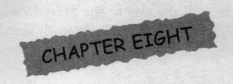

CHAPTER EIGHT

"I've been waiting for you." Jessie fell into step with Rockett the next morning outside school.

"Then you're not mad at me anymore?" Rockett asked hopefully.

"I've got this problem," Jessie said, sidestepping the issue. "Ginger's asked me to play flute with her bagpipe number."

"Tell her she can't!" Suddenly, Darnetta was beside them. "We had her first and anyway, she can't change her mind in the middle of auditions."

"Why can't I play with both of you?" Jessie asked Darnetta.

"Tell her, Rockett," Darnetta demanded.

"Tell her what?" She wasn't even inside the building and already there was a new problem to solve. Rockett rummaged through her backpack for the tryout schedule. "Okay, Ginger's moved to . . . this afternoon."

"I know. We practiced last night," Jessie told her. "Anyway, 'Netta, you've got Viva and Ginger's got no one."

"But I asked you first and you said yes," Darnetta protested.

They made it all the way to the front door before the next catastrophe caught up to Rockett. It was dressed in standard Ones gear: designer labels from headband to shoe leather.

"Are Cleve and Max in the show?" Stephanie demanded. "I mean, they may not be the comedy duo of the decade, but they are my best boy buds."

"I don't know," Rockett confessed. "I don't think Ms. Tinydahl and Mr. Baldus have made final decisions yet."

"'Cause I want them in my act," Stephanie continued.

"You want Tinydahl and Baldus in your act?" Ruben joined the group surging in the front door.

"Duh, like right, Ruben. They'd just be perfect. Not. I was talking about Cleve and Max," Stephanie said.

"What happened to you last night?" Ruben asked Rockett. "You were supposed to get back to me."

"To do what?" Darnetta said.

"'Netta, that's none of your business," Jessie whispered.

"I was talking to Stephanie," Darnetta objected. "I'm just wondering what Max and Cleve would do in a bird act."

Rockett ran through a bunch of excuses but couldn't decide on one Ruben would buy. Finally, she said, "Actually, I was so tired, I just decided to chill. I'm really sorry —"

"*De nada* — as long as you're gonna go to bat for me with Ms. T."

"Well, here's the thing," Stephanie gushed. "You

know Panama can say like yes-and-no stuff. So I made up this list of *hysterical* questions that Cleve and Max can ask him and then he'll answer!"

"Ruben, I . . ." She stopped and turned to Stephanie. "Stephanie, that's a classic idea!"

"It so is! Look, I brought the questions." The gifted Ones girl thrust a bulky pile of paper at Rockett. "They're so fun."

Wow, finally, someone's got a solution, not a problem!

"So what's your decision?" Darnetta was back on the case. "Can Jessie switch sides?"

"Can't I be in both?" Jessie asked again.

Sure, Rockett was about to say. Then she thought, *I'd better check with Ms. Tinydahl.* "I don't know," she confessed. And a voice in her head — that sounded so like Nicole's — went, *Wuss!!*

"You *are* gonna read my questions, right?" Stephanie insisted.

"Um, sure." Rockett flipped eagerly through the pages. "Is blue your favorite color? Is it red? Is Mr. Baldus a good homeroom teacher? Do you like milk?"

Hysterical? So fun?

She can't be serious. These queries go from dull to lethal. We'll need an emergency team to revive the audience.

"Gee, um, how many questions were you planning to use?" she asked cautiously.

"All of them!" Stephanie squealed, psyched.

Rockett's heart sank.

I can't tell her how bad this is. I mean, at least she tried.

85

But it would be way worse to let her audition bitterly boring material.

They were in the hallway now, near the eighth-grade lockers. Ruben peeled off toward his. "Catch ya later," he said. "Just remember, I'm countin' on you."

"You haven't told him yet," Jessie noted.

"What?" Rockett said, still lost in the parrot jungle.

"Ruben. You know he can't end his act with an electrical explosion. Ms. Tinydahl would never —"

"I'm doing the best I can, Jessie," Rockett snapped. "This whole dumb thing of me being stage manager was your idea —"

"Hello — a smile? A giggle? I am so waiting." Hands on her hips, Stephanie was staring at her. "I stayed up half the night thinking up comical questions, and now you go all coma-girl on me?"

Rockett was regretting her outburst, feeling helpless as Jessie hurried away with Darnetta at her heels.

"Can we talk later, Steph?"

"Way later," the bitter girl barked, snatching back her pages and taking off down the hall.

What was that? I haven't even made it to homeroom yet, and everyone is mad at me or — like Ruben — is gonna be.

"I sense your pain with every follicle of my being."

Like a golden mirage in a desert of defeat, Rockett saw Mavis moving toward her.

"I am sooo glad to see you!" Rockett greeted the approaching prop-girl-to-be. "Mavis, I'm really sorry about what happened yesterday —"

"You mean the manner in which your banana-brained associate insulted me?"

"I promise you," Rockett said passionately, "it won't happen again."

"What won't?" Arnold asked, strolling toward them. He seemed not to have noticed Mavis glowering at him. "Have you spoken to you-know-who about you-know-what?" Glancing around to be sure Whitney wasn't near, he finally spotted the scowling seer.

"Well, well, it's mighty mouth," Mavis scoffed. "The reeking rodent king of the planet cheese breath!"

"Arnold, don't!" Rockett warned. But it was too late.

"Well, well, break out the dancing teacups. It's Beauty . . ." he said, looking from Rockett's pleading face to Mavis's vengeful glare, "and the *Beast*."

"Arnold, apologize. Please," Rockett urged. "I just told Mavis you'd stop being so —"

"Pathetically dumbo!" Mavis finished for her.

"— insulting," Rockett amended. "I promised her you'd stop. I gave my word!"

"Well, your mouth is writing checks your body can't cash," Arnold grumbled.

"Mavis, please, please, will you do prop chores for the show?" Rockett asked, stepping between them.

"Not until you muzzle Zit-wit, the wonder dog!"

"You're calling me a dog?" Arnold sneered. "Takes one to know one, Fido-face."

"Don't you dare say one more word, Arnold," Rockett raved, "or you are so out of the show!"

Kids had heard the ruckus and stopped in the hall. They faced her now, some gaping, some gasping, some going, "Oooooo." Only one was smiling — Nicole!

Like twin comets, Arnold and Mavis streaked off in opposite directions.

"Problems?" Nicole purred, stepping out of the crowd to put an arm around Rockett's slumping shoulders.

"Did you see what happened?" Rockett babbled miserably.

"Who didn't?" Nicole said.

"I mean, what was I supposed to do? I need Mavis to help with the props, and Ms. Tinydahl assigned Arnold as my assistant, but he can't stop dissing Mavis and, well, I'm, like, stretched thin on all fronts, but I guess I shouldn't have threatened him that way. It just popped out. And everyone's all mad at me. This is so hard, Nicole. Like, duh, who knows that better than you, right?"

Nicole removed her comforting hand as if it had been resting on a trash pile. "Excuse me?" she said coldly.

"Well, I just mean, all the problems you had last year, you know?"

"Problems? What problems? *I* never had any," Nicole asserted.

"No, but you know, how everyone was so steamed at you . . ."

"As if!" Nicole sneered. Then she turned on her chunky heels and stalked away.

Could I be any dimmer? With everything crashing around

me, I turn to Nicole for emotional support? And how do I try to bond with her — by reminding her of last year's talent show debacle and all the kids who so painfully panned her!

Of course, she went into frantic denial — just like I'll be doing next year!

The bell rang.

Help, it's only time for homeroom. Could this day get any worse?

It could.

Despite her ducking and hiding all morning, Arrow nailed her at lunchtime.

"You never e-mailed me," the irate archer accused.

Rockett mumbled an apology. "I haven't had time to straighten things out with Wolf," she said. Then, desperate to avoid Arrow's wrath, she went, "Whoops, there's Ms. Tinydahl."

"Where? I don't see her," Arrow said.

"She just walked out of the cafeteria. I've gotta catch up with her." Rockett raced for the lunchroom door — and crashed into Ms. Tinydahl, who was just coming in.

"How is everything going, dear?" the teacher asked as Nicole and Stephanie passed them.

"Fine," Rockett squeaked, feeling Arrow's baffled gaze burning her back.

"All set for today's auditions, Rockett?"

"I don't *think* so," Nicole crooned in an amused singsong, "but I am, Ms. T. You are so going to love my reading."

"Especially if you remember to bring a blanket and

pillow to tryouts," Sharla jeered as Ms. Tinydahl left them. "I picked up a copy of *Negotiating Kindergarten* at the drugstore. They shoulda sold it in the sleeping pill section."

Sharla wasn't that far off.

During Nicole's reading, kids squirmed, crackled wrappers, yawned, and coughed. No matter how hard she tried, the vivacious leader of The Ones could so not pump excitement into *Negotiating Kindergarten to Win*.

It was just hard to get cranked about "friendship quotients" and "actualizing playground popularity" and "exercising interpersonal approval potentialities."

"Thank you, Nicole," Ms. Tinydahl called politely over the boos and rude noises that followed the presentation.

The CSGs tracked onto the stage in soccer gear. Dana, the best player on the Starfire team, led her buds through a series of rhythmic ball-passing moves. "It'll be way better when we've got music behind us," Nakili explained after missing one of Miko's passes.

Rockett cheered them on. "I totally give them points for originality," she told Ms. Tinydahl.

Sharla was up next. Dressed all in black, she perched on a stool to recite the epic poem she'd written especially for the show.

". . . So while we bay at the pale moon, in the gloom of homeroom like a broom Mr. Baldus sweeps our tomb," she recited.

"Very nice, dear," Ms. Tinydahl said encouragingly.

90

"I thought it was an obvious suck-up to Mr. B," Stephanie consoled Nicole.

It was Ginger's turn. Jessie had gotten permission from Mr. Baldus to accompany her. But the wailing, moaning, and screeching Ginger managed to coax from her uncle's bagpipe caused a run on aspirin during their performance.

At the end, only Darnetta looked happy and migraine-free. Jessie looked thoroughly blue.

"You sounded really good," Rockett tried to assure her.

Jessie didn't even look up. She just shrugged. "I only hope I didn't ruin Ginger's chances," she said, leaving the stage.

Wow, Jessie's really down. I wanted to cheer her up, but did she even hear me? Well, if she did, she probably didn't believe me.

I mean, why should she? I haven't exactly been all tell-it-like-it-is this week. Jessie knows that better than anyone.

But soon so will Arrow and Ruben and Wolf and Whitney.

"I don't want to talk to anyone," Rockett told Juno when she got home. "So if you're still expecting a call, you answer the phone, but just say I'm . . ." She made vague motions with her hands. "Whatever."

Juno was at the computer again. She had barely looked up when Rockett walked in. Now she spun around on the desk chair.

"Wow," she said, studying Rockett, who'd flung herself backward onto her bed. "You look like I feel."

*Oh, really? What's that supposed to mean? Is Juno hurtin'
on the inside or am I lookin' cool on the outside?*

"Rough one?" her sister asked.

*Okay, I guess I'm lookin' and she's feelin' . . . bummed?
Could it be true?* Rockett propped herself up on her el-
bows. *Is my flawless sister having a rotten day?* "How about
you?" she probed.

"Ugh." Juno made a face. "I asked you first."

"Me? I'm okay." She was getting pretty good at dodg-
ing the truth. Too good, actually. "I mean, you know, not
bad."

"Not bad is good, I guess," Juno noted. "Me, I didn't
get the call I've been waiting for."

Hello, was this her big sister — expressing something
less than total confidence and joy? Could Juno actually
be blue? If so, they had lots more in common than a
set of parents. Weary of pretending, Rockett decided to
level. "Actually, I'm more not good than not bad. Which
call — Josh?"

"Yep. I feel like such a jerk, mooning around waiting
for a guy to phone. What's your excuse?"

"This stage manager thing," Rockett confessed. "I
thought I'd be so good at it. But I'm like this total loser,
snapping at friends, embarrassing kids. Lying," she finally
said. "I mean, they're not evil lies or anything. They're
just not to hurt people's feelings —"

"'Cause you want them to like you?"

"Well, yeah. Is that so bad?"

"Only if you feel you have to lie to get them to."

"It's just hard to say no when kids ask you for stuff. Or they want your opinion and it's one you know they're not gonna like."

Juno shrugged. "I totally relate. I mean, like, 'No is a complete sentence.' I like that idea, but it's hard to do, right?"

"Yeah, tell me about it," Rockett said, teasing. But then she sat up. "No, seriously," she said. "Tell me about it. I really need help."

It was that easy.

The way lying had become routine, telling the truth — that one simple sentence, *I really need help* — seemed to be habit-forming, too. After she said it, more and more truth spilled out.

She talked to Juno about Jessie, about Wolf and Arrow, and Ruben . . . and about how trying to help Stephanie had caused a chain reaction that left Whitney without an act . . . and about how she'd messed up with Arnold because he'd messed up with Mavis. . . . And how she sided with Ms. Tinydahl about Ruben but not about Viva's costume.

"I really need help," she'd said, and help Juno did.

The phone rang several times while they talked. They both looked at it, but didn't pick it up. Their mother took messages. And by the time Juno wound down, there were lots of them — but none from anyone named Josh.

If that still bothered Juno, you sure couldn't tell. She

was like totally in teacher mode, focused on Rockett's issues, grilling and drilling her on how to go from stressed-out stooge to stage manager supreme.

"So okay," Rockett said just before their dad knocked on the door and asked them to come out for dinner, "let me do this back to you. You said that, um, learning to say no . . . you know, but doing it courteously —"

"Politely but firmly," Juno prompted, "without insulting anyone or trying to justify your opinions . . ."

". . . is tough," Rockett continued. "And, like, it might make me unpopular in the short term."

"But . . ." said Juno.

"Yeah, but it'll earn respect and keep my dread and distress level way down."

"Ta-da, little sister. The truth will set you free!" She and Juno slapped a stinging high five. "Getting kids to work together is hard, too —"

"But that's how it's got to happen," Rockett said, all pumped now.

"You're gonna totally go under unless you get people to cooperate with one another and start to seriously delegate responsibility," Juno reminded her. "And that means Mavis and —"

"Yeah, I know, Arnold, too."

"It's hard but that's what's got to happen. Think you can move Mavis past her injured pride?" Juno asked.

And convince Wolf to help Arrow? And get Whitney to work with Arnold?

"I'm gonna try." *With Mr. Baldus and Ms. Tinydahl's*

help, Rockett thought. *That's what Juno meant by "managing up" — which is another skill she thinks I need to work on. Like getting teachers to help out when there's a problem. And being "persistent" — staying on them until they get what I'm saying.*

"How come you know all this stuff?" Rockett asked as they headed for the dining room — where, hopefully, their mother had cleared the table of the boxes of fabric and paper, twigs and shells she used in her collages.

"Trial and error." Juno grinned. "Lots and lots of error."

She probably studied all this stuff in college.

Confession Session

The bagpipe is way harder to play than I thought. But I loved doing it. A little more practice and I'd be really good. I know Jessie and I didn't make the cut, but there must be some way we can still do our Irish duet. Maybe Rockett'll have an idea. She's so creative.

I dreamed of me and Wolf last night. Chanting. Dancing. We were playing this big old drum together, like an upside-down washtub, all decorated with fur and feathers and beads. And then the whole class got up and sang with us. It was cosmic.

On Saturday morning, the school was nearly deserted. The sound of Rockett's footsteps echoed off the metal lockers lining the halls.

She was feeling way lighter today. As if, literally, a weight was off her. Thanks to Juno, who'd kept pushing her to just do it, she'd reached most of the kids on her list last night.

Turning the corner, she noticed someone rummaging noisily through a locker. As she drew closer, Rockett saw that it was Mavis.

"Hey, I tried calling you last night, but your phone was busy. What are you doing here today?" she asked. "You're not auditioning, are you?"

"Ha-ha. As if. I'm looking for something," Mavis said sheepishly. "There's this rhinestone headband I picked up at the RagBag. It's really like this fake old tiara, you know. But it'd be perfect for Zeit-banana's assistant — whoever the unlucky girl turns out to be."

"You're helping Arnold?"

"No way! I'm helping this extremely needy and amateur so-called talent show."

"Mavis, I mean, I know Arnold upset you —"

"Even when he called me to apologize last night he upset me!"

"Arnold called to apologize?!"

Rockett had asked him to — politely, courteously. Then she'd ordered him to. And, when he'd continued balking, she'd begged. And the bullheaded brainer had actually done it! Rockett was astounded.

"But I cannot let him stand in my way," Mavis went on. "I am the best finder of funky old clothes and fabulous accessories in this entire school and probably in the state, also. It's a gift. Ah-ha! Here is the crown!"

She showed Rockett a sparkling, slightly bent tiara studded with yellow rhinestones. "Mavis, you're amazing. It's perfect! It's just like the one in the picture Arnold gave me."

"Yes, I had this rather twitching vibration about it," Mavis said almost shyly. She squeezed shut her crammed locker. "Well, you hold on to the headband. I'm off to find Darnetta's song."

Yesss!! Rockett fairly skipped down the hall, twirling Mavis's excellent tiara.

"Yo, wait up!" It was Ruben, with his guitar case slung over his shoulder. Wolf was with him, pushing a huge wooden box on wheels. They caught up and walked alongside her.

Ruben did not look happy. "So when am I doing this sliced-and-diced version of my solo?"

"I don't know yet," Rockett confessed. She wished he

wasn't so bummed. All she'd done last night was tell him the truth, that she agreed with Ms. Tinydahl, that she thought blowing up anything in the auditorium was whack.

"Don't you want to know what's in the box Wolf's wheeling?" Ruben challenged.

"Hey, Rock." At least Wolf wasn't mad at her. She'd explained everything and apologized to him last night, and then, using Juno's cooperation speech, she'd tried to talk him into working with Arrow. "I've been thinking on it" was all he'd said.

Now he was grinning — and looking good, Rockett thought. She'd never seen his long black hair braided.

"You speak to Arrow yet?" he asked. "I mean, did you straighten her out that this whole powwow idea was strictly yours?"

Rockett sighed deeply. That had been the hardest phone call. "Omigosh, he must've thought I was mental!" Arrow had groaned. "He had no idea what I was talking about, right?"

"Yes," she answered Wolf. "I told her last night."

"Are you talking about me?" Arrow said.

Rockett jumped and clutched her heart. "I totally didn't hear you coming," she gasped.

"Moccasins." Arrow pointed to her feet. "Very quiet. For sneaking up." She laughed.

Arrow was in a really good mood. Rockett was surprised but relieved.

"Amps!" Ruben said sharply. "In the box," he explained when she blinked cluelessly at him.

"You're going to go through with it?" she asked, shocked. "Ruben, you can't. It's dangerous. Plus you'll get in a lot of trouble."

"Psych out!" he laughed. "Gotcha, suckah."

"That is so not funny," Rockett grumbled.

"Naw, there's no amps in here. It's just drums," Wolf said.

Ruben cracked up laughing.

"And that's not funny, either," Rockett scolded. "In fact it's way insensitive."

Didn't Wolf remember that Arrow was standing right there? Didn't he realize how badly she'd wanted to team up with him for a drum duet? She did not find anything amusing about Wolf pretending there were drums in the box.

Unless he wasn't pretending?

"What's going on here?" she asked.

"Ooooo, don't make the stage manager mad," Ruben teased.

"I told you last night I was gonna think about it. And I did," Wolf said. "Don't laugh, but I even asked the Great Spirit for a sign —"

"Yeah, and then I had this excellent dream about us doing our powwow thing," Arrow added. "Isn't that spooky? And I called him this morning —"

"So we're gonna give it a shot. I got a load of my grandpop's stuff in here. Really neat Pawnee stuff."

"It was a great idea, Rockett," Arrow said, giving her a deluxe bear hug. "Wish us luck."

When they got to the auditorium, Jessie and Ginger were waiting.

"Thanks for the phone call last night," Jessie said first thing. "It really made my night. How far down the list did you get?"

"Well, you were the first," Rockett said.

"Hey, you didn't call me," Ginger pretended to complain.

"You were one of the lucky ones," Rockett teased, "who I didn't have anything to straighten out with or apologize for — I hope!"

"Naw, if anything," Ginger said, blushing, "I should have apologized . . . for that weak performance yesterday. Guess I need some bagpipe practice. Which I'm totally committed to doing. I was working on it last night."

"Which is when she got her neat idea. Tell her about it, Ginger," Jessie prompted.

"Well, actually, it was Arnold's," Ginger corrected her. "After that lame tryout yesterday, he asked if I'd be his assistant. I could tell he was only being nice. It was so obvious that my playing didn't make the cut. Even *Arnold* felt sorry for me."

"And everyone knows he really wants Whitney to do it," Jessie added.

"So when I said no thanks, he went, like, there really ought to be a way for kids who don't make it into the talent show to still be able to perform. You know, 'cause of all the hard work everyone does to prepare and all."

"That's an awesome suggestion," Rockett agreed.

"So I was thinking, maybe we could put on, like, an alternative performance; you know, like losers of the talent show unite!"

"Cut that out. You are so not the loser," Jessie told Ginger.

"Just kidding. But how about if we did a really informal show just for kids in the school. You know, no parents, no outside audience —"

"Like maybe in the cafeteria one lunch period," Jessie offered.

"Cool," Rockett agreed. But she was thinking, *I wish there was some way everyone could be onstage the night of the show*. She pulled the clipboard out of her backpack and jotted a note on the audition schedule. "I'll check it out," she promised.

"Great," Jessie said. "Have you seen Stephanie's parrot yet?"

Stephanie, Cleve, and Max were huddled at the back of the auditorium.

"How's it going?" Rockett asked.

"Well, it was nice of you to call and all, but we still don't have an act," Stephanie said, looking sadder than her droopy parrot. "I mean, okay, so my questions weren't fabulous."

"They were as bright as Alaska in December," Max grumbled.

"Not even," Panama squawked.

Rockett and Max laughed.

"I'm with the bird," Cleve said. "Man, our jokes were better than those questions."

"I don't think so," Panama blurted.

"That bird is funnier than our jokes," Max noted.

"He is pretty funny. But you know, I really liked some of your jokes," Rockett told the boys.

"Yeah, name one," Cleve challenged.

"Like where you said, 'I took an IQ test and the results were negative —'"

"Way!" the bird said.

"Hey, cut it out," Cleve teased Panama. "When we want your opinion, we'll ask for it, okay?"

"Not even!" Panama crowed. The bird that had been hunched over on its perch was all puffed up now.

Stephanie noticed it, too. "Look at Panama. He's practically his old self again. He's loving the attention."

"Omigosh! That's it. It's perfect! Guys, I think you've got an act," Rockett said, suddenly psyched.

Max caught on right away. "We tell bad jokes, and the bird acts like a critic, right? He disses us."

"Way!" Panama chimed in.

"That's hysterical!" Stephanie said.

"Not bad," Cleve decided.

"I don't think so!" the parrot proudly squawked.

Rockett was on her way to the stage, to talk to Ms. Tinydahl, when Arnold cornered her. He was wearing his magician's costume, a full-length wizard's robe with wide sleeves, which were making cooing noises and kept flapping.

"My doves," he explained when Rockett stared at his fluttering arms. "I did everything," he hissed. "I swallowed my pride and my breath mints and phoned Mavis Wartella-Depew and, though I can hardly believe it myself, I apologized to that mental midget."

"I heard," Rockett said. "And now she's our prop girl and look what she gave me." She showed him the tiara. "For your assistant."

"What assistant? Do you see an assistant? I don't see an assistant," the boy ranted. "I see Whitney Weiss sitting in the front row, chatting with her close personal adviser. I did what you wanted, Rockett, and what have I got to show for it?"

"I'll talk to Whitney again," Rockett promised.

"What's it worth to you?" Suddenly, Nicole had joined them.

"Everything, anything!" Arnold blurted. "Can you talk Whitney into working with me?"

"Of course," Nicole said. "But I want to emcee the show. I want to be the Mistress of Ceremonies and introduce the acts."

Yesterday, Rockett realized, Nicole's demand would have so flipped her out. She'd have tried to find fifteen ways to make it happen. Today, she wondered what Juno would do — or Jessie — and it got simple.

"Mr. Baldus is emceeing," she pointed out.

"He didn't audition," Arnold cried. "Everyone else had to audition, why doesn't he?"

"Because he just doesn't, Arnold. He's a teacher. He always emcees the talent show," Rockett said. "But maybe he wouldn't mind letting Nicole introduce a few of the acts."

"How few?" Nicole wanted to know.

"I'll have to talk with him," Rockett said, "but maybe he'll consider it. Did you see the tiara Mavis scored for Arnold's assistant?" She showed the glittering headpiece to Nicole.

"Very princess. Did she mug a trick-or-treater to get it?" Nicole snatched the tiara and looked it over. "Not bad," she concluded. "Okay, you take care of Mr. Baldus, and I'll get Whitney pumped for magic."

"Goddess!" Arnold cried, falling to his knees before Nicole.

"Yuck," she said, and walked away.

"Rockett, are we ready?" Ms. Tinydahl called.

"Got my clipboard right here," Rockett answered. "Can I talk to you first, though? You and Mr. Baldus. There are some . . . issues, I guess . . . that I need your help with."

Viva was first on her agenda. It was time for Ms. Tinydahl and Mr. Baldus to move into the twenty-first century.

"I just want to say again, Ms. Tinydahl, that I really like Viva's dance costume," Rockett told them when they huddled in the wings. "But if you guys think it's too clingy or whatever, I'm gonna suggest that Viva ties one of her sheer scarves over it. Something airy and light that floats like her Indian print skirts and gauzy blouses."

Mr. Baldus raised his eyebrows questioningly at Ms. T. The English teacher took a moment, then nodded at him.

"Done," Mr. Baldus boomed. "The sheer scarf'll do it. Next case."

"Oh, thank you, thank you, thank you," Rockett couldn't help squealing. Then she cleared her throat and glanced at the pad she'd taken notes on last night. "Ruben Rosales has cut his solo to five minutes — with no explosive ending or anything. So would it be okay for him to have the final spot in the show, you know, play the finale? I think he'd do an excellent job."

"Let's put that decision aside until everyone's had a chance to audition and we know what the final lineup of acts looks like," Ms. Tinydahl said.

"But we'll certainly take your opinion into account," Mr. Baldus promised.

"Cool," Rockett agreed. "There's other stuff that we don't have to do right now. Except for one thing" — she cleared her throat — "it involves . . . well, actually, lots of kids — Nicole, Arnold, Whitney, Mavis, Stephanie . . . me . . . Actually, it's kind of about class unity and harmony and putting on a really tight show that everyone can feel good about and participate in."

She took a breath. And then did her best to explain how Arnold had forced himself to apologize to Mavis so that she'd agree to be prop girl and that he had his heart set on Whitney being his assistant, which, in Rockett's opinion, was such a phat plan since Whitney hadn't been able to put together an act because Rockett had ruined her and Nicole's tryout idea by talking Stephanie into doing something with her depressed parrot — so really, it was all her own fault, she had to admit, and she took, like, total responsibility — but everything could work out if Mr. Baldus would just be willing to share his Master of Ceremonies chores with Nicole.

The teachers looked at each other when Rockett finished.

"I'm not sure I understand," Ms. Tinydahl finally said.

"I think I do." Mr. Baldus hesitated. "*Think* being the operative word here. You're askin' me — for the sake of our show — to let Nicole introduce the acts."

"Just a couple of them," Rockett said.

"Groovy. Why didn't we think of that before? More students would be able to participate if we had them introducing the different acts."

"Why don't we try it with Nicole this year," Ms. Tinydahl suggested.

"I'm down with that," Mr. B agreed.

"Speaking of participation." Rockett saw her chance. "This is just an idea. I mean, Ginger and Arnold came up with this cool way for more kids to showcase their talent in a lunchtime show. But I'm thinking, in addition to that, what if we had this grand finale onstage and everyone who tried out for the talent show — whether they made the cut or not — could participate in it?"

Mr. Baldus was delighted. "Participation! That's the key to it all," he enthused. "Don't you agree?" he prompted his colleague.

"It is, indeed," Ms. Tinydahl admitted. "Very creative, Rockett. I think we can manage it. Is there anything else?"

She thought about it. *Here goes*, she decided. "Well, I just wanted to say that, well, um, when you guys decided to give me an assistant — I wish you'd have talked to me about it before you just did it, you know?"

"Point well taken," Ms. Tinydahl said stiffly.

"She means, we'll chew that one over for a while," Mr. Baldus translated with a chuckle.

"Whew," Rockett said, "that was a chore. But, I've gotta also admit, Arnold turned out to be kind of okay."

Rockett couldn't wait to get home to tell Juno how well it had gone. She ran into the house, flushed with success.

But Juno was so not where Rockett expected to find her. She was not on Rockett's phone, not on Rockett's computer, not in Rockett's room.

"Where's Juno?" she asked her mother, who was working on a watercolor still-life in the dining room.

"Shhhhush. She's resting," her mother answered.

"Resting? It's, like, the middle of the afternoon. Is she sick again?" Rockett asked.

"No." Her mother sloshed her paintbrush around in the water jar and, for a moment, watched the color swirl. "She's just disappointed . . . and sad."

"Juno? Get out. What's she got to be sad about?"

"Rockett," her mother said sharply. "What kind of question is that?"

"Well, I just mean . . . I wasn't trying to be mean."

"Why don't you go talk to her," her mother suggested. "She's lying down in my room."

Rockett tapped at the door. "Juno? Are you okay?" she called, then tiptoed in. "Are you sleeping?" she whispered.

Juno had a pillow over her head. She rolled over, knocking the pillow to the floor. "No. Just hangin'," she said. "Wussup?"

"Well, not you," Rockett said gently. "What happened?"

"Ask me what didn't happen," Juno said.

And Rockett knew. "The phone call?"

"Bingo! Josh never called. He said he would. He said he'd drive down from school, and we'd hang out this weekend."

"Wow, you must really like him," Rockett blurted.

Juno smiled. Then she scooched over and patted the bed and Rockett sat down next to her. "What's crazy is I don't. I mean, not enough for it to feel so rotten that he didn't call. I don't even know for sure what happened. Maybe he tried —"

"Oh, no, you mean when I was on the phone last night? Oh, wow, I was on for hours. I didn't realize."

"No. I don't think that was it," Juno assured. "I mean,

we do have call-waiting. But speaking of you and the phone — how'd it go today?"

"Sooooo fantastic!" Rockett squealed. "I had, like, such an excellent day. You just wouldn't believe it."

"Try me." Juno sat up, propping pillows behind her back. "Give me the blow by blow."

Rockett was about to let loose, but she stopped. It was like, *click.*

"What? Why are you looking at me that way?" Juno asked, smiling nervously.

Suddenly, Rockett grinned, too. "Oh, no," she said. "I'm not gonna blow this chance. You totally saved me last night. You're always helping everyone else. Now it's my turn!"

"You're wiggin', little sister. What are you talking about?" Juno wanted to know.

"You. Let me do something for you for a change. Please, Juno. I'm sorry you're down, but —"

"What, you're so glad I'm human?" Juno laughed.

"Totally!"

Juno shook her head. "Okay, you're on. I'll take a pot of herbal tea. A couple of the wickedest cookies you can find. And, let's see, then I want you to tell me everything about your day — especially all the parts where I was right!"

"No problem," Rockett said, "if you promise you'll come back to see the show!"

Confession Session

Hi, I'm Nicole! Welcome to the most fun talent show since mine last year. No. Um, welcome to the second-best talent show ever! That'll be better. Okay, now give it up for my golden homey, Whitney, who will be strutting the runway in a vintage spangled suit . . . oh, yeah, and, like, handing magic stuff to Arnold, whatever. I, your gracious emcee Nicole Whittaker, present a bevy of my very best buds, Cleve, Max, and the incomparably jiggy Stephanie — tellin' bad jokes and cheerin' up birds! I was so born for this job.

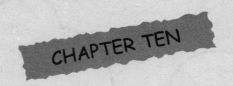

CHAPTER TEN

Rockett paced backstage, clipboard in hand, checking on a hundred little things that didn't need checking on.

The sets, which she, Nakili, and Darnetta had helped to design, were perfect. Dana, whose father was a carpenter, headed the construction crew that built them.

Chaz, the coolest guy in The Ones and Nakili's fantasy squeeze, had the lighting chores under control. While Bo, who balked at everything but computer lab, was running the soundboard like a pro.

And true to her word, Mavis had come up with the choicest props and costumes ever. The show was in progress. Nicole was onstage introducing Sharla.

So there was nothing for the stage manager to do.

"You look way professional, Arnold," she whispered, passing the busy boy.

He was wearing his worn purple-velvet wizard's robe over an everyday T-shirt and jeans.

"Thanks," he mumbled, focused on giving hand signals to his dove.

"So you're all set to go on after Stephanie?" she asked him for the tenth time.

He had said yes the first nine times. Now he just ignored her and went back to trying to make the bird disappear. The white dove just sat in its box staring at him.

Rockett wandered over to where Jessie and Darnetta were watching Viva do her warm-up exercises.

"So Mavis gave you the music?" she whispered to Darnetta.

"Right here." Darnetta waved the same sheet of paper she'd shown Rockett five minutes ago.

"And, yes, Rockett." Jessie held up her flute. "I've still got my instrument."

"Okay, then. Just checking."

"Rockett?" Viva straightened up.

Rockett spun toward her eagerly. "You need something? You didn't sprain your ankle, did you?"

"I just wanted to say thanks again."

"Oh," Rockett said. There was no emergency. Nothing to do. "You're welcome," she mouthed.

She moved on, glancing out at the stage.

Sharla was performing now. Hunched on a stool in her black leather jacket, the girl was somberly reciting her gloomy opus.

Rockett had recommended that Stephanie's act follow the dark poet for comic relief.

"Everyone all set?" She hurried over to where Max and Cleve were quietly going over their jokes with Stephanie and Panama. The parrot was preening happily, ready for his showbiz debut.

"Excuse me, could you swing by here one more time before we go on?" Stephanie whispered.

"Yeah, 'cause that'll make it an even dozen," Cleve kidded her.

"I just want to know if you're ready," Rockett protested.

"Way!" Panama squawked exuberantly.

"It's just that we're running a little late because of Nicole's introduction —" Rockett said.

"I thought she did very well," Stephanie rushed to her friend's defense.

"Yeah. Why'd Sharla get so snarly when Nicole called her poetry tormented?" Cleve asked.

"No, she said *demented*," Max told them. "Whoops, Sharla must be done. I hear a little applause and a lot of nose blowing."

"Go, go, go!" Rockett shooed them toward the stage.

"What's the hurry?" Cleve asked. "Nicole's gotta introduce us."

'Yeah, that'll give us about . . . an hour," Max estimated.

Rockett rushed to the edge of the wings and tried to signal Nicole.

"So help me welcome three of my close personal friends, who are so devoted to me," Nicole was gushing. "And one fabulous parrot that made the most amazing comeback in show business history. You're gonna love little Panama, which Stephanie got when she was just a little girl trailing me around grade school. Panama is a special bird — to all of us . . ."

"Thanks for helping Nic get the job." Whitney,

sparkling in rhinestones, gold, and glitter, was suddenly standing beside Rockett. "She really needed the ego boost."

"I don't think so!" Panama squawked.

Nicole heard him and glanced their way. Rockett tapped her wristwatch, trying to signal the chatty One that she was going way overtime.

"Well, our stage manager — whom I personally recommended for the job — is telling me that the show must go on!" Nicole announced, ambling toward the wings. "So here they are now, without any further ado, my own best buds . . . the Parrot People!"

Stephanie and her crew ran past Rockett onto the stage.

"How excellent was that, Rockett? How I, like, gave you that plug." Nicole breezed into the wings.

Ruben, Wolf, and Arrow were on the other side of the stage.

Arrow's lookin' so chill in her Cherokee beads, Rockett was thinking, when the proud girl caught sight of her — and threw her a humongous grin. Rockett sent back a thumbs-up sign. Then Wolf noticed her and elbowed Ruben, who winked at her.

Rockett felt herself blush. Turning away, she saw Ms. Tinydahl beaming at her.

"You've done a wonderful job, Rockett," the teacher said. "There's nothing left to do now but relax and enjoy the show."

"That's an order," Mr. Baldus added.

Hidden behind the curtains, she watched as Stephanie, in a sassy stage voice, said, "You know, you have to stay in shape."

"Yeah. My grandmother started walking five miles a day when she was sixty," Cleve responded.

"She's ninety-seven today," said Max, "and we don't know where she is."

"Not even!" Panama squawked.

A new wave of laughter rocked the audience. Rockett peeked out at them, hoping to see Juno.

She didn't, couldn't. The auditorium was too dark.

But she did catch sight of her mother and father. Sitting in the second row, they were dimly visible in the light that spilled from the stage. They looked like they were lovin' the show.

"Cleve," Max announced as soon as the laughter died down, "I think you got into the gene pool while the lifeguard wasn't watching."

"Way!" Panama screeched.

"If I gave you a penny for your thoughts, Max," Stephanie said, "I'd probably get change back —"

"Not even!" the parrot raved.

"You guys were wicked," Whitney informed her buds as they tore off the stage to thunderous applause. "I only hope we do as well."

"I'll trade you birds," Arnold offered, holding out his dove box.

"Okay, Mr. Baldus is finishing your intro," Rockett told them. "Good luck. Go, go, go."

Arnold raced for the stage, then turned and raced back to Rockett. "Did I say thanks?"

"You did," Rockett told him. "Did I?"

"Probably. But I can stand it if you want to tell me again."

"Thank you, Arnold. You are an epic assistant and a mega-magician!"

"I know," he said, grinning wildly. "You heard her. Let's go, Whitney. We're gonna kill 'em!"

They nearly did.

Arnold's oversized deck of cards, which Whitney handed him with an elegant little twirl, shot from his fingers again.

"Duck!" Max hollered from the wings and the first three rows cringed, dodged, crouched, covered their faces, or fled their seats. Then everyone, including Rockett's parents, just cracked up. And they kept laughing. Especially when Arnold's white dove just sat perched on the inept magician's fingers, refusing to disappear.

Finally, Whitney, all squeamish but determined, plucked the stubborn bird from Arnold's hand.

"I will now make this dove disappear," she announced, and carried it into the wings, where Stephanie gently took it from her.

The failed magic act drew surprisingly loud applause. Arnold and Whitney took their bows, and Mr. Baldus announced a short intermission.

The lights went up. Rockett hurried around the back

of the stage, eager to get out front to meet her parents. But it was Juno she was thinking of.

Was her sister over her Josh heartbreak? Or too blue to keep her promise to come to the show?

"Rockett!" her parents called as she burst through the backstage door. "This is wonderful. We're having such a good time."

"Too bad Juno couldn't come," Rockett said glumly.

"Are you kidding?" her father said. "She's here. She wouldn't have missed it."

Her father pointed up the crowded aisle. Rockett saw her sister weaving her way toward them. With a tall hottie following closely behind her.

Juno gave her a big hug. "Wow, this is even better than I imagined," she said. "That last act was hysterical. We got here a little late and had to sit way in the back, but what we've seen is choice."

We? Rockett smiled up at Josh. *So he called, after all. Duh, of course. This is Juno we're talking about. My brilliantly talented sister. Who wouldn't call her?*

Juno saw her staring at the boy.

"Rockett, this is a friend of mine from school," she said. "Stephen, meet my brilliantly talented little sister."

Stephen?

Whew. Not only does Juno heal fast, she recovers in total style! And — did I hear right — did Juno just call me her brilliantly talented sister?

Rockett started to laugh. "I'm sorry, Stephen. I thought you were — um, someone else," she tried to say.

Juno shot her a warning look, then she started to laugh, too.

"Mr. and Mrs. Movado?" Mr. Baldus joined them. "So are you folks down with the show so far?"

"Very much," her father assured him. "It's terrific, fast, funny . . ."

". . . and groovy?" Mr. Baldus suggested.

"That's it, exactly," Rockett's mother said.

"Rockett, can you sit with us for the second half?" Juno asked.

"Gosh, I don't know . ."

"Of course. Of course!" Mr. Baldus assured her. "Hang with them. What've you got to do backstage?"

Go mental? she almost said. *Drive everyone crazy?*

"You can see everything much better out here. Go, enjoy!" he insisted.

The lights dimmed. Her sister took her hand, and they hurried back with Stephen to their seats.

Rockett could barely sit still through the rest of the acts. They were amazing. Each one more fun than the next.

Wolf and Arrow's drumming and chanting brought the entire audience to its feet.

The "Delta Girl Blues" Project was the bomb! Viva's sheer, sassy scarf floated and fluttered as if enchanted by Jessie's lyrical flute and Darnetta's strong, silky voice.

And when Ruben stood alone in the final spotlight, making his electric guitar do earsplitting, mind-boggling riffs, people started hollering, whistling, and stomping as if they were at a rock concert.

Finally, he pulled the plug on his amp and, in the wild applause that followed, the entire talent show crew stormed onto the stage — the kids who'd performed and the ones who'd only tried out and the behind-the-scenes crew.

Rockett saw Ginger pulling Mavis from the wings. The CSGs started tossing their soccer ball around. Mr. Baldus took Nicole's hand and they bowed together. Max and Cleve pulled Ms. Tinydahl onto the stage. The audience stood and kept clapping as they took bow after bow.

Then Ms. Tinydahl looked around at all the kids.

"We're missing someone," she said. "Rockett Movado, our stage manager. Where's Rockett?"

"Right here!" Juno's friend Stephen shouted.

"You'd better get up there, Rock," her sister said.

So she ran to the stage. Hands reached down — Ruben's, Arnold's, Arrow's, Jessie's — and pulled her up.

Rockett stood for a moment, glowing, happy, proud, surrounded by all the kids who'd made the talent show happen.

Then everyone started applauding again. The audience, Ms. Tinydahl and Mr. Baldus, the kids onstage . . .

And suddenly, Rockett wasn't standing anymore.

She was soaring into the air as her grateful classmates, shouting and cheering, lifted her onto their shoulders for a rousing curtain call!

Rockett's World™

GET READY!
GET SET!
READ ROCKETT!

$3.99 US each